AF538932

LOVE IN ANCIENT INDIA

LOVE IN ANCIENT INDIA

M. L. VARADPANDE

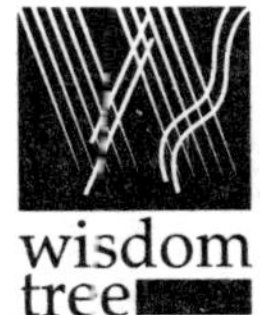

First published 2007

ISBN: 81-8328-050-1

Published by
Wisdom Tree
4779/23, Ansari Road,
Darya Ganj,
New Delhi-110002

Published by Shobit Arya for Wisdom Tree; *copy edited by* Swapna Raghu Sanand and Manju Gupta; *designed by* Kamal P. Jammual; *typeset at* Marks & Strokes, New Delhi –110028 and *printed at* Print Perfect, New Delhi -110064

रतिचक्रे प्रवत्ते तु
नैव शास्त्रं न च क्रमः
— वात्स्यायन

Ratichakre pravitte tu
naiva shastram na cha kramah
— Vatsyayana

(When the wheel of Kama
is set into motion,
there is then
no *Shastra* and no order!)

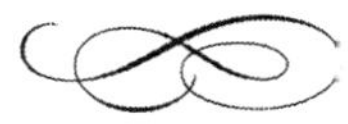

Contents

A *delighted* nayika *eagerly waiting for her lover*

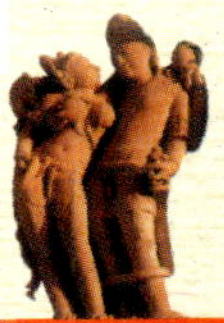

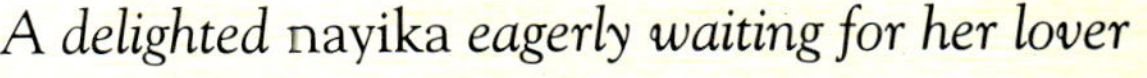

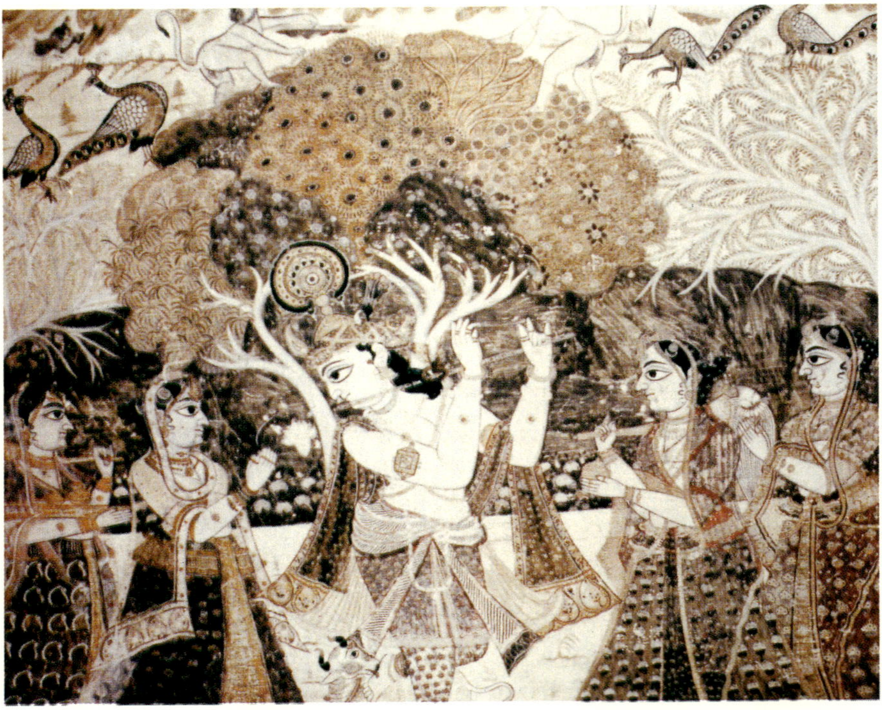

Krishna playing the flute under a tree while the gopis *surround him*

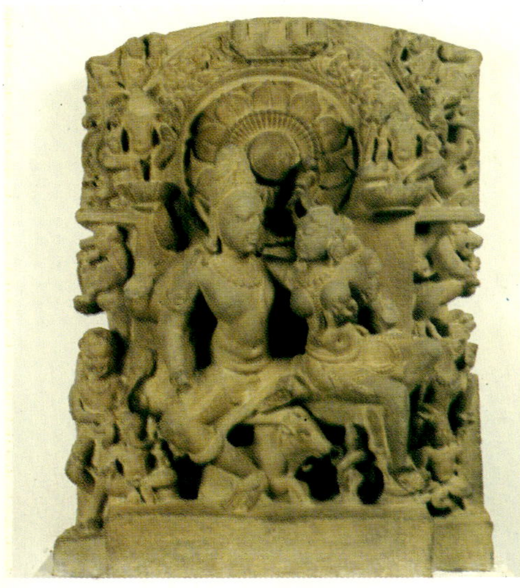

A stone sculpture of Uma-Maheswara in an embrace

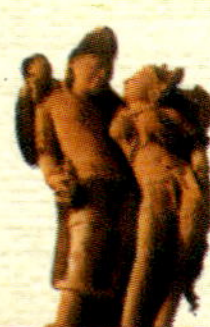

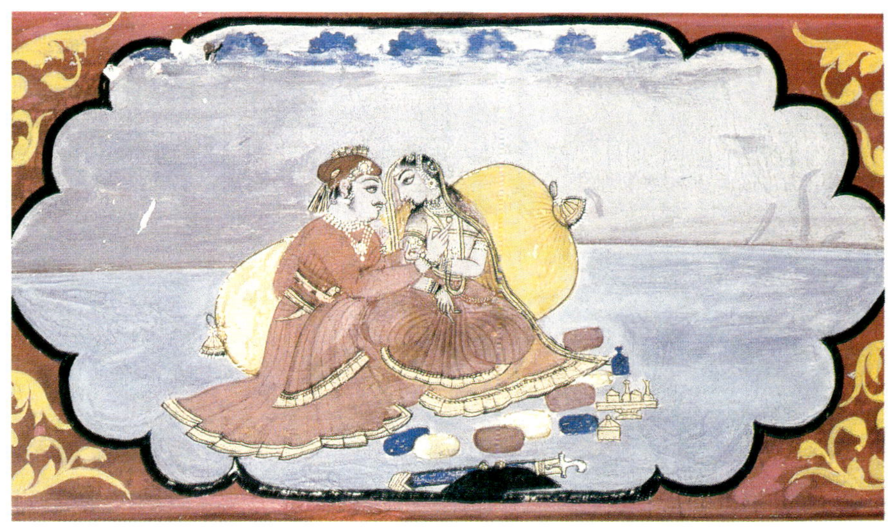

A nayak *and* nayika *sitting coyly*

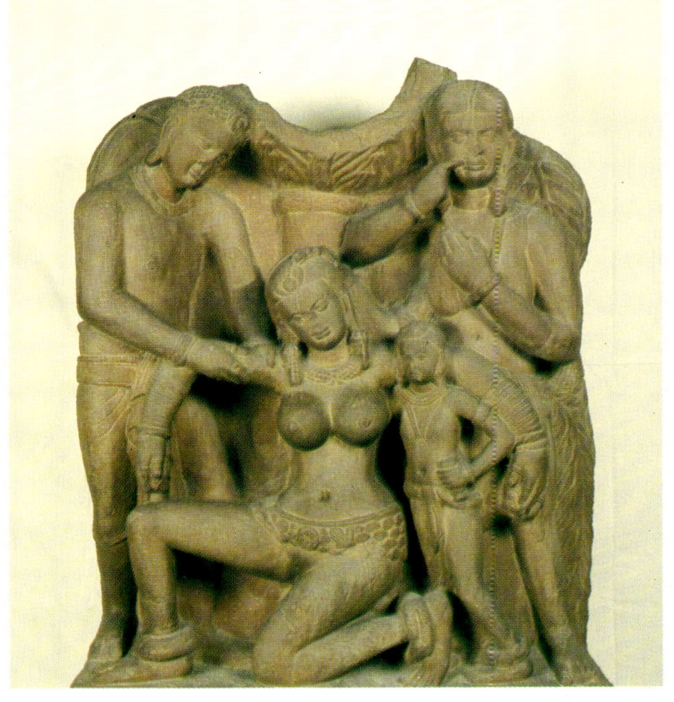

A sculpture depicting a scene in a courtesan's house

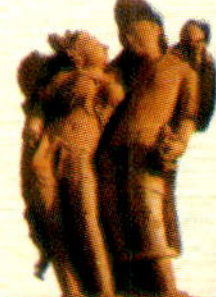

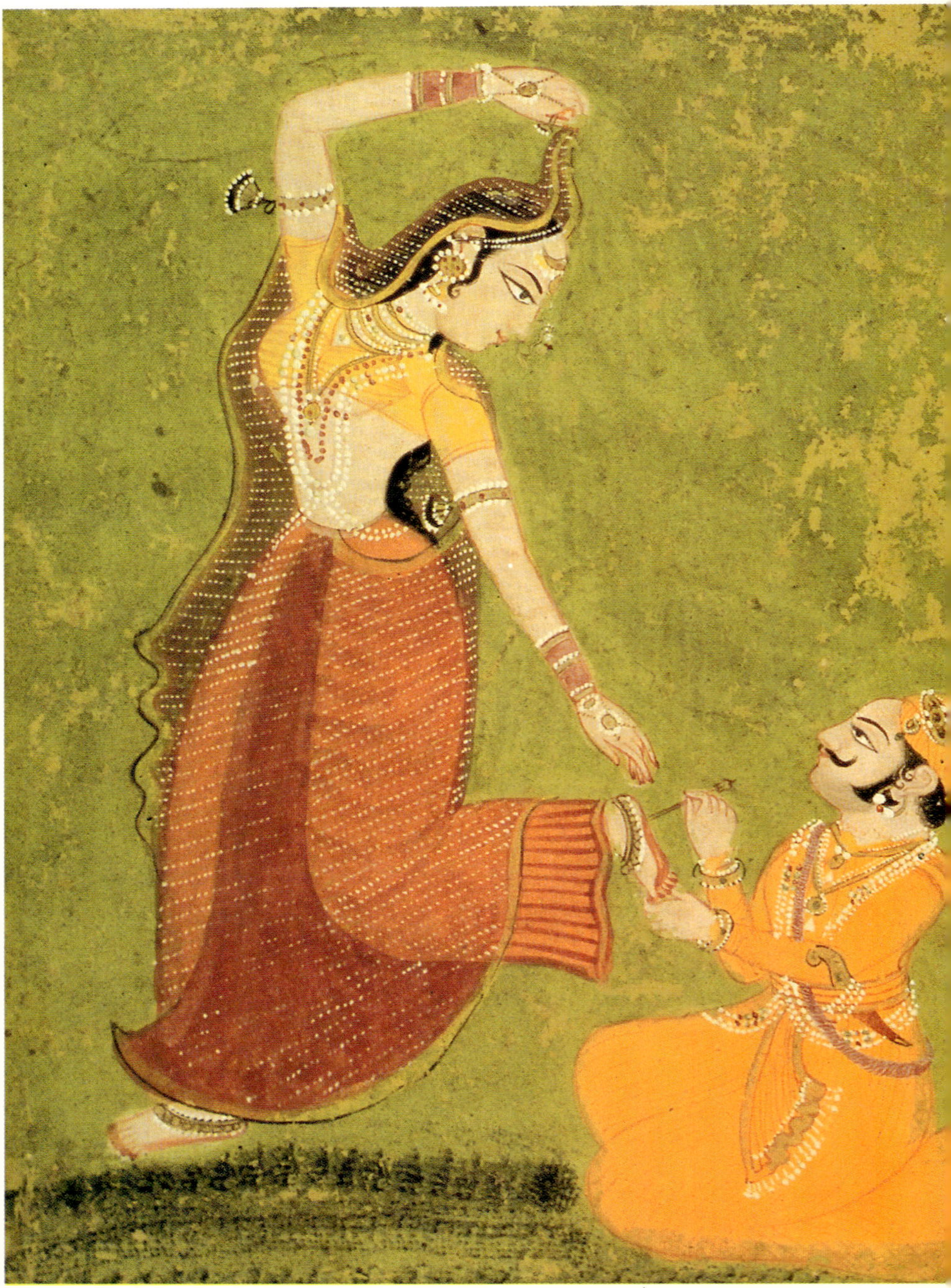

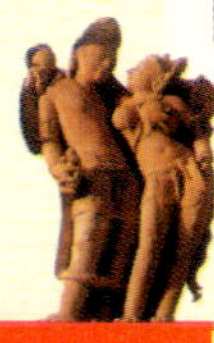

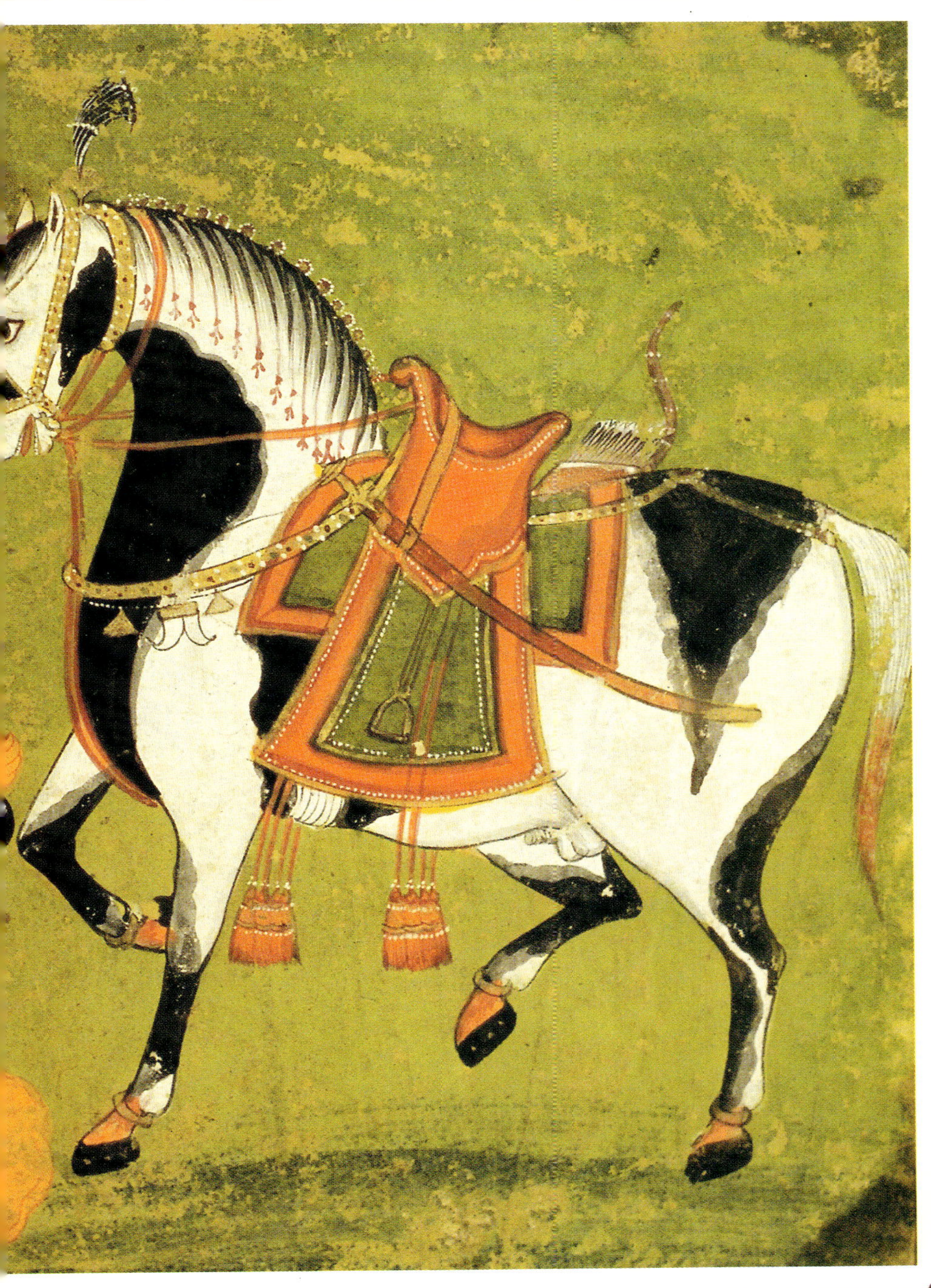

A nayak *removing a thorn from the foot of the* nayika

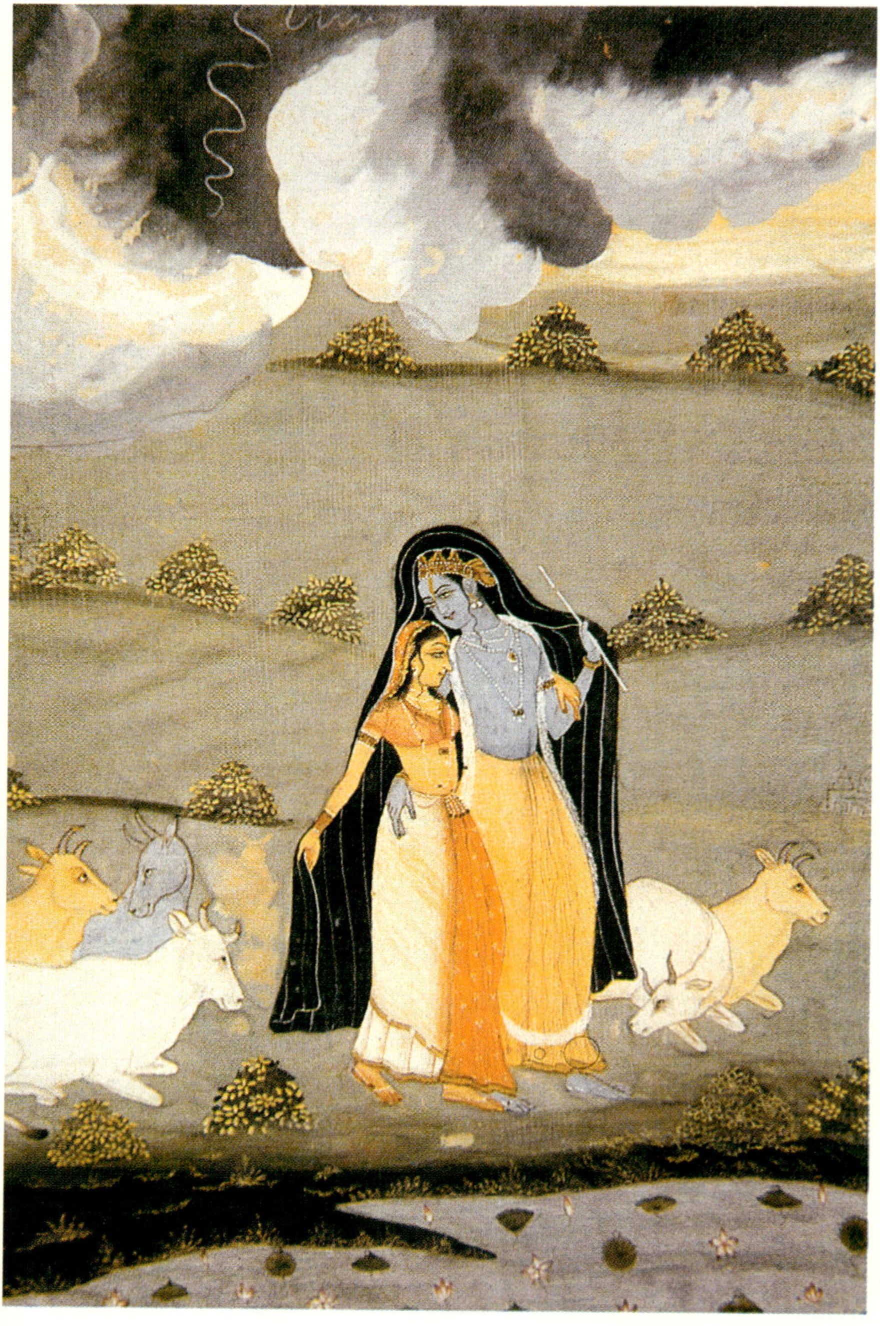

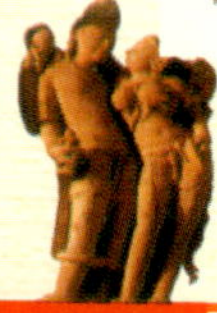

Radha and Krishna sheltering each other from the rain

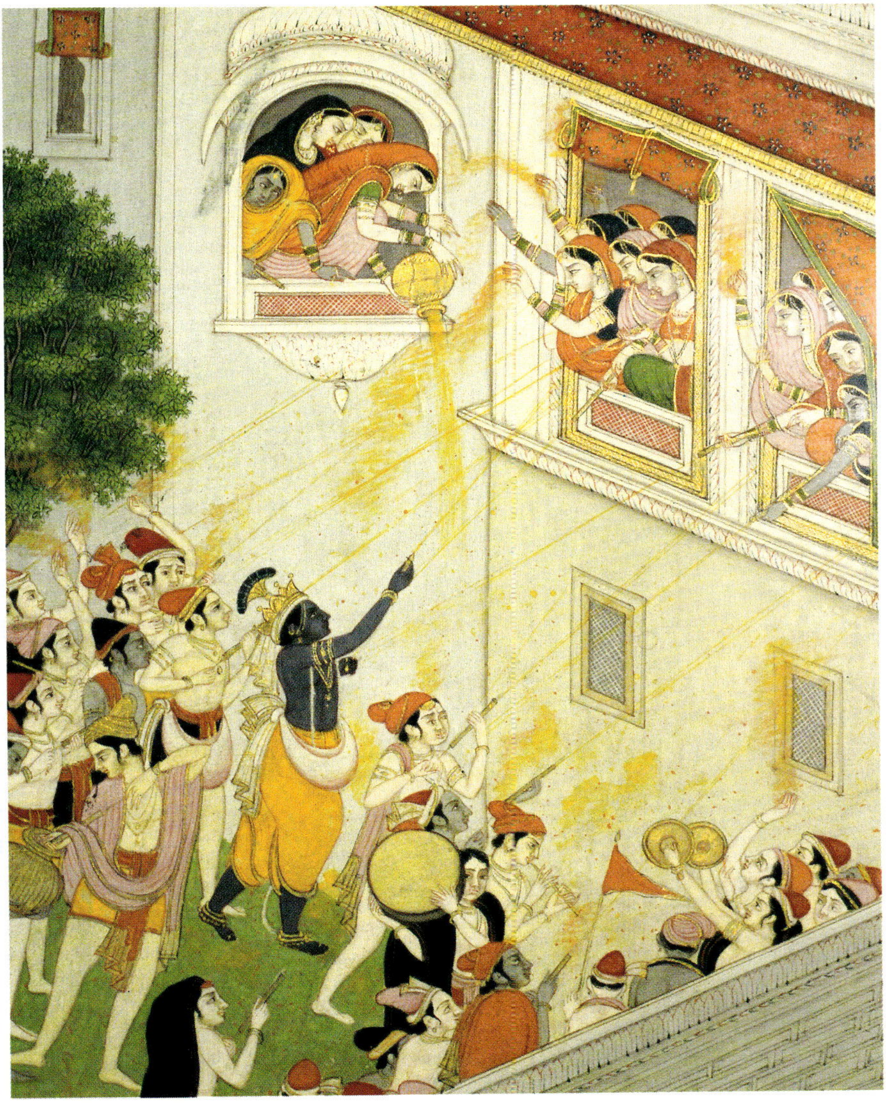

A prince playing Holi *in his harem*

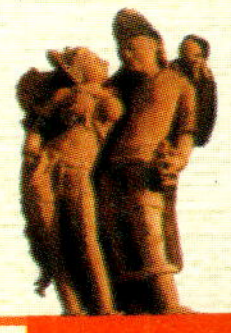

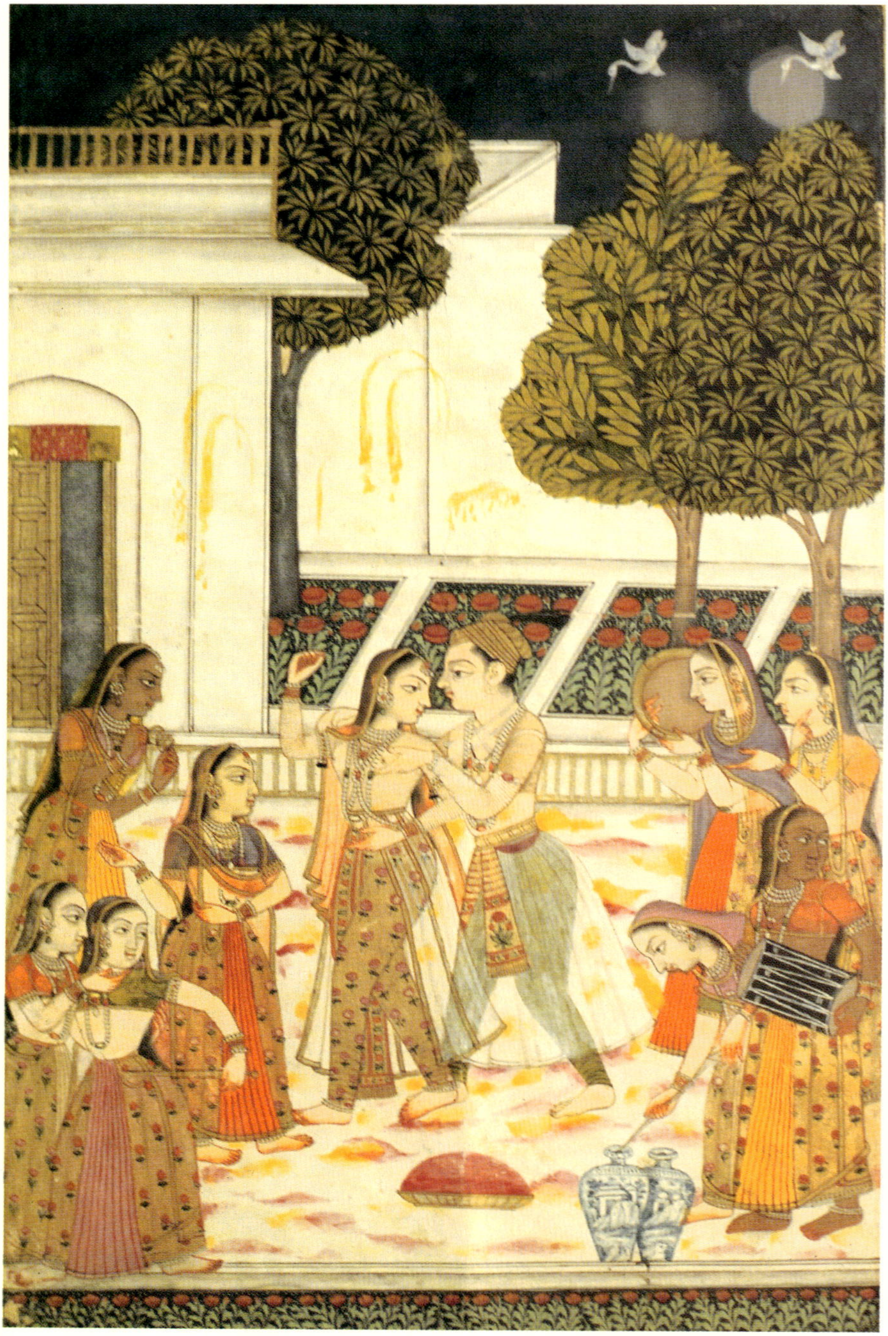

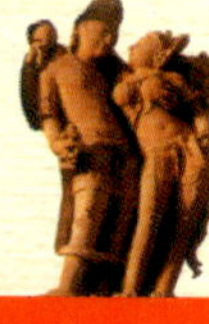

A pair of lovers embracing while the maids wait to sprinkle coloured water on them

Chapter One

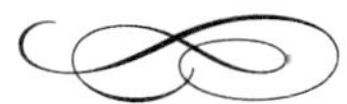

God of Love

Indian mythology considers Kama as god of love. Kama literally means lust, passion, desire, sexual longing, sensuality, pleasure and enjoyment. Kama, the god of love, is all these things personified.

The ancient Indian books of knowledge, *Vedas*, say that Kama was born at the beginning of creation. He is described as virility of mind, *manaso retah*. The arrow of the god of love is described in a hymn of *Atharva Veda* as one having wings of mental agony. Its shaft is made of a wish to enjoy carnal pleasures, *samkalpa*. The metal point of this shaft is the desire to make love, it says.

The above-mentioned hymn in the *Atharva Veda*, with Mitravarum and Kamabana as its deities, is a kind of magic spell used to seduce a woman and make her yield to the desire of her lover. In the same *Veda*, there are three hymns dedicated to deity Smara, who is none else but Kama.

The word *kama* as the desire to share bed with one's lover has been mentioned well before the *Atharva* and the *Rig Veda*. A dialogue-hymn in *Rig Veda* involving Yama, the first ancestor, and his twin sister Yami, is full of passion. Yami implores Yama to make love to her. She says:

> The desire, *kama*, of Yama has approached me, Yami, to lie with me in the same bed. Let us exert ourselves in union like two wheels of a chariot.

Vatsyayana is the author of the world famous classic, *Kamasutra. Kamasutra* defines *kama* as a tendency of the five sense organs, propelled by the mind to beget pleasure, *pravritti.*

> *Sparsha* (touch) is the sphere of skin, *shabda* is (sound) of ear, *rasa* is (savour) of tongue, *rupa* is (form and colour) of eye, *gandha* is (fragrance) of nose.

The pleasure of *kama* is highest as it involves all the five sense organs which transmit favourable sensations to the mind and ultimately to the soul. It is both a physical as well as spiritual experience, Vatsyayana says.

A number of mythical stories about the birth of Kama are found in later literature. Generally he is considered to be the one who sprang from the mind of Brahma, the lord of progeny. *Kalika Purana* gives the story of the birth of Kama quite elaborately, weaving it into a number of mythological tales. He, however, retains his Vedic character as a deity of love carrying the bow and arrows. At the National Museum in New Delhi, there is a terracotta plaque from Kaushambi attributed to the second century BC. Here, the lovers are seen sitting side by side in very close proximity on a chair. The entire background is covered with a floral design. Flowers are suggestive of spring, *Vasanta ritu,* as it is considered a friend of Kama. Obviously, the man depicted thus is none else but Kama and the woman is his consort, Rati.

The Government Museum at Mathura has a standing, headless, male figure made of baked red clay. In his right hand is a cluster of arrows while in his left, he carries a beautiful wreathed bow. Traditional ornaments and drapery on the body are remarkable. The background is beautifully decorated in attractive floral designs. The figure is identified as that of Kamadeva. Under his left foot lies the figure of a man who is identified as a fisherman named Surpaka. Kamadeva is shown turning the heart on Surpaka in favour of Kumudvati, who loves him intensely.

According to an ancient legend, Princess Kumudvati became attracted to a fisherman, *minaripu* named Surpaka but he did not desire her. Ultimately, Kamadeva made Surpaka fall in love with the beautiful princess.

Ashvaghosha, an ancient author, was one of the contemporaries and spiritual advisor to King Kanishka in the first century of our era. A brief mention of this legend of Princess Kumudvati is found in Ashvaghosha's epics entitled *Saundarananda* and *Buddhacharita*.

Bhana is an interesting form of drama — a monologue delivered by a single actor, *eka-nata nataka*. The basic theme of *bhana* plays is the life of the courtesans. Their locality was known as *vesha* or *veshyavat*. We start getting *bhana* plays since the Gupta period.

In *bhana* play, *Padmaprabhrutakam* by Shudraka, written in the Gupta period, there is mention of a play entitled *Kumudvati Prakarana,* which is based on this story related to Kamadeva. Courtesan Devasena was in possession of the script of the play written on palm-leaves as she had been selected to play the role of Kumudvati. Kama was a favourite god of the courtesans. No wonder the enactment of plays based on legends related to him constituted a common theme in those days.

King Hala Satavahana of Paithan compiled about seven hundred Prakrit verses in the second century AD. The collection became famous as *Gatha Saptashati*. There are a number of *gathas,* verses, related to Kama. His various names, such as Ananga, Madana, Manmatha, Smara, are mentioned in these verses. His love arrows are frequently mentioned; even the festivals held in honour of Kama are mentioned. A *Gatha* says:

> Hair disarrayed by the touch of a lusty lover and mouth fragrant with the scent of wine — this much make-up is enough for a young, beautiful girl to attend the festival of Kama.

Kama's name as *Makaradhwaja* too is mentioned; *makara* means crocodile. The flag of Kama bears the symbol of a crocodile. It was believed that the crocodile was sexually the most potent animal.

According to a legend recorded in the *Rati Rahasya*, the bow of Kamadeva was made of sugarcane and had a string of bumble bees lined together. His five arrows were respectively made up of five kinds of flowers, *navamallika*, Ashoka, mango blossom, blue lotus and red lotus. The parrot and the pigeon were counted among his vehicles. The fragrant flower-buds of mango and the clusters of blossoms were considered arrow-heads of Kama's deadly arrows.

Thus, we see the myth of Kama growing over the passage of time. Many interesting legends were woven around him. Temples, *Kamadevayatana*, were built in honour of Kamadeva. One such temple in Ujjayani was very famous and finds mention in literary works such as *Kadambari* of Banabhatta and plays like *Mricchakatika* and *bhana Padmaprabhrutakam* by Shudraka.

In *Padmaprabhrutakam*, Vanrajika, the beautiful daughter of a courtesan, Vasantvati, is described as descending gracefully down the steps of the temple of Kamadeva after offering worship to the deity. She had decorated her body with flowers that blossomed in spring, *Vasanta ritu*. It seems that courtesans used to offer special worship to Kamadeva during spring.

In the *Bhana* play, *Padataditakam* of Mahakavi Shyamilaka, the Kamadeva's temple is mentioned twice. In the play, there is a reference to an old courtesan, who after offering worship to Kamadeva in a temple, circumambulated a pole bearing the flag of Kama carrying the crocodile symbol, *makarayasti*. It seems that such a pole existed in front of the temple and it was customary to circumambulate it. In the premises of the temple, she saw hungry crows attack the food offerings made by the devouts and a dancing peacock, also. The temple was located where the courtesans resided.

In Banabhatta's *Kadambari,* we are told that on the housetops of Ujjayani, the *makarayasti*, fluttered, conveying that in the city, Kama was a favourite deity.

In *Mricchakatika* by Shudraka, there is mention of the temple of Kama and of a beautiful flower garden in front of it. It is told in the play that for the first time the heroine of the play, the courtesan called Vasantasena, sees Charudatta, a young, handsome but a poor Brahmin, in the garden in front of the Kamadeva temple and falls in love with him. Obviously, courtesan Vasantasena must have gone there to offer worship to Kama in his temple. This also implies that Charudatta was like the other young boys who must have been loitering in the garden attached to the temple in the hope of catching a glimpse of the beautiful courtesans living in the city of Ujjayani.The autumn festival, called the *Vasantotsava*, full of fun and frolic was being celebrated in honour of Kamadeva. The people are depicted as singing, dancing, drinking wine and indulging in all sorts of pleasures on the occasion.

Emperor Harsha, who transferred his capital from Thaneshwar to Kannauj, was a noted author and playwright. He wrote three Sanskrit plays — *Nagananda, Ratnavali* and *Priyadarsika*. In *Ratnavali,* he describes the autumn festival as *Madanamahotsava,* the festival of Cupid. In the first act of the play, we see *varavilasinis,* courtesans totally drunk, singing and dancing happily.

During the ninth century, Damodar Bhatt in his famous work, *Kuttanimatam,* tell us that courtesans of Varanasi used to enact the first act of Harsha's *Ratnavali* in the temple of Kashi Vishwanatha.

In the *Ratnavali,* we find Queen Vasavadatta worshipping the image of Kama (Bhagavan Pradyumna) placed under an Ashoka tree in the royal pleasure garden. After that she is seen offering worship to her husband King Udayana. As a gift, she gives flowers, ornaments and *vilepana,* a fragrant paste for applying on the body, to Vidushaka, who is a Brahmin. Princess Sagarika, who watches the ceremony while hidden behind some trees, remarks that the painting of Kamadeva is worshipped in the harem of her father.

Writing about *Vasantotsava* in his book, *Festivals of India,* Dr B.N. Sarma says:

> King Harsha in *Priyadarshika* and Dandin in his *Dashakumarcharita* state that on a full-moon day, an image or picture of Madana, the god of love, was placed in a garden under an Ashoka tree, and its trunk decorated with saffron fingerprints. The deity was then worshipped with offerings of flowers, turmeric, perfumes, rice, silk cloth, etc. Subsequently, married women began to perform the worship of their husbands in almost the same manner. At times, even princes went out to join in the *Vasantotsava* celebrations in the gardens outside the town, in the company of their beloveds. On this auspicious occasion, the Brahmins were given presents of various kinds for attaining religious merit.

The tenth century work *Kavyamimamsa* of Pandit Rajashekhara states that during *Vasanta ritu*, women worship Gauri while dancing and singing songs, enjoying swinging on swings and participating in a number of merriments. Siddharsi Suri (AD 905) has given a vivid description of this festival in his work, *Upamitibhavaprapanchakatha*. He says that swings were hung in the gardens and Kamadeva was worshipped by young women who wanted fulfilment of their desires. While virgins prayed to the god in the hope of getting suitable husbands, married women worshipped to secure longevity of the life of their husbands. Amorous men, desirous of having relations with women, also went there to worship Kamadeva. Idols of Kamadeva and his consort Rati, sleeping on a cushioned bed with pillows, were worshipped by women.

Srinarmanjirikatha of the Parmara king, Bhoja, mentions this festival as *Yatramahotsava* of Madana. Jimutavahana, a great jurist of Bengal, refers to this festival as *Kamamahotsava*. He also states that on this occasion, the people used objectionable expressions to the accompaniment of music, because they felt that by such a practice Kama was propitiated and cajoled into conferring wealth and progeny on his devotees.

The Prakrit work, *Akhyanakamanikosa* of Acharya Nemichandra Suri states in that maidens worshipped the *makaradhwaja* to get husbands of their choice.

Banabhatta, a Sanskrit scholar and court poet of Emperor Harsha, is also notable for writing one of the world's earliest novels, *Kadambari*. In the fourth chapter of Banabhatta's *Harshacharita*, there is description of a honeymoon chamber designed for a newly married couple. On the entrance gate of this chamber, paintings of Kama's wives, Rati and Priti, were drawn. According to the *Matsya Purana*, Kama had two wives — *Pritih syah dakshine tasya; Ratishchya vama parshve tu*). In the Mandsor inscription by Bandhuvarma, Kamadeva is mentioned along with his consorts, Priti and Rati. Inside the chamber, on the wall was a painting of Kamadeva standing under a full-blossomed Ashoka tree with an arrow on his bow, ready to shoot, is depicted.

Devangana Desai in her *Erotic Sculpture of India,* writes that Chhinamasta, a fierce *tantric* goddess, has to be visualised, according to *Mahakalasamhita,* with Dakini and Varini on either side and Rati and Kama involved in the pose, woman on top of man, *viparitarata* at her feet.

She further writes in *Naishadhacharita:*

> In the twelfth century, Sri Harsha gives a vivid description of the royal palace which had erotic depictions. The recreation hall of the princess's palace, in her father's palace where she stayed before her marriage, had depictions of a pair of lovers. In the inner apartment of the main palace were idols of Kamadeva and Rati. On the walls of the palace were depicted amorous paintings and sculptures with themes taken from mythology. The adulterous frolicking of Indra with Gautam's wife was engraved on the wall. At another place, Kamadeva laughs at Brahma's rash passion for his own daughter.(p.116)

According to the *Mahabharata,* a son was born from the chest of Lord Brahma and was named Dharma. Dharma had three sons, namely, Sama, Kama and Harsha. Of the three, the exceedingly handsome Kama became the god of good looks and passion. Rati became his wife.

In the opening chapters of the *Kalika Purana,* the legend of Kama is narrated. During the course of his creation, Brahma brought into being an exceedingly beautiful girl, Sandhya. She was very fair, *arakta gaura,* with eyes like full-bloomed blue lotus and the gait of a deer. Her bosom was very attractive and rounded, *pinottunga,* and waist very thin — so thin that one could hold it in a fist. She was slim, *tanvi,* lovely to look at, displaying an enchanting smile on her lips, *charuhasini.* The ample hair on her head was naturally blue and feet very red.

When Brahma, the lord of creation, looked at her with great fascination and carnal longing, a youth sprang from his mind with a floral bow and arrows in his hands. Obviously, Brahma's passion took the form of a handsome youth called Kama. When the youth asked Brahma what his *kama* was, Brahma ordained him the task of making men and women fall in love and be helpful in the work of creation. From his breath, Brahma created *Vasanta ritu* to help Kama. Kama used his deadly arrows on his father himself and made him fall in love with the lovely Sandhya.

According to *Brahmanda Purana*, when Brahma fell in love with his own daughter, he sensed it was a prank played by the mischievous Kama, whom he cursed that he would be killed by Lord Shiva, the destroyer of evil.

One of the most famous Puranic legends about Kama is his burning down by Shiva and has been very poetically rendered by Kalidasa,one of India's greatest poets in his epic poem, *Kumarasambhava*. The poem captures the wedding scene and the union of Lord Shiva and Parvati in the immortal verses penned by Kalidasa. The birth of their son, Kumara Karthikeya who is born to destroy the demon Taraka is a focal point in this poem.

The demon Taraka became very powerful and drove gods out of their heavenly abode, the *swarga*. The gods approached Brahma, requesting him to come to their succour. Brahma told them that the son born to Shiva and Parvati would lead the army of gods as their commander and vanquish the demon.

However, Parvati, the beautiful daughter of Himalaya and Mena, was not yet married to Shiva who was immersed in deep meditation in the lofty Himalayan region. Everyday, Parvati worshipped and served Shiva with love and devotion but the latter took no notice of her as he was too deeply engrossed in his rigorous penance, *tapas*.

Indra remembered Kama, who instantly appeared before him with an arched bow as beautiful as the curved eyebrows of a young woman, and slung over his shoulder. He carried an arrow of mango blossoms in his hand.

Kama boastfully asked Indra to assign him any task as he could accomplish it within no time. Indra asked him to make Shiva fall in love with Parvati. With his friend Vasanta, Kama went to the spot where Shiva was seated. Vasanta, by magic, made the tree blossom with flowers all around. But when Kama saw Shiva immersed in complete absorption of the soul, *samadhi;* he lost his courage and his bow and arrows fell to the ground. But when Kama saw the beautiful Parvati approaching him, courage returned to him.

Meanwhile Shiva came out of his meditation. His attendant Nandi, a bull, informed him about the arrival of Parvati. The great lord invited her to his presence. She respectfully offered worship to him. Kama seized this opportunity and placed his flowery arrow on his bow to shoot at the *yogi*, Shiva. Suddenly Shiva felt the stirring of passion for the lovely Parvati. Surprised by the sudden awakening of lust in his mind, Shiva controlled his emotions and started looking around for the cause of his mental disturbance. Shiva's gaze then fell on Kama who was about to shoot his arrow at him. Shiva flew in a rage and opened his fiery third eye. A column of fire emerged out of his third eye and struck Kama, reducing him to ashes.

Soon after Shiva disappeared from the scene along with his *bhuta ganas*, Kama's wife Rati started weeping inconsolably on seeing her handsome husband turned into a fistful of ash. A divine voice from the sky said that it was all due to Brahma's curse that Shiva would vanquish Kama.

After the burning by Shiva, Kama acquired a new epithet — one without the body, *ananga*. But this did not diminish his power to make a man and woman fall in love with each other. On the contrary, his ethereal existence helped him to quietly accomplish his task by remaining invisible to the eye.

Kama, in due course, was reborn as the son of Krishna and Rukmini and was given the name, Pradyumna. When he was just ten-days old, the demon, Shambara picked him up from his palace and threw him in the sea, where a fish swallowed him. It so happened that some fishermen caught this fish in their net and sold it to Shambara's cooks, who slit open the fish. To their surprise, they found a child inside its stomach.

Rati, wife of Kama, had already taken birth as Mayawati and was in the employ of the demon. She took charge of the infant, who soon turned into an exceedingly handsome young man. Mayawati told him that in her previous birth she was his wife. Pradyumna killed the demon Shambara and returned to his parents in Dwaraka with his wife.

The *Bhagavata Purana* gives a new dimension to the Kama legend by stating that he was, in fact, a part of Vasudeva Krishna — *kamastu vasudevansho.* After he was set on fire by Shiva, he turned to Krishna to be allowed to take rebirth.

Indian ascetic schools consider Kama as the first and foremost of *shada-ripus,* the six inner foes or faults of man, viz. *kama, krodha, lobha, harsha, ahankar* and *mada.* Lust and desires destroy man. Summarising various ascetic theories, J.J. Meyer, author of *Sexual Life in Ancient India* says:

> Indeed Kama is an ally of Mrityu, god of death. Apart from the destruction it otherwise brings, it is also *samsarhetu,* the cause of continuance of this world of pain and death. Overwhelmed by passion, man is dragged about by Kama, bringing anguish, joy and sorrow and suffering in its wake.

Delightful, naughty, erotic and even obscene in parts, the festival of Holi is related to the Kama legend, of his burning by Shiva. This legend of destruction and resurrection of Kama is celebrated in the form of Holi festival.

Basically, Holi is celebrated for two days in the month of *Phalguna.* On the day of the full moon, *Purnima,* the ritual of bonfire signifying burning of Kama is performed in the evening and the next day is devoted to boisterous revelry which includes singing, dancing, music, drinking, intermingling of men and women without inhibitions, throwing of coloured powder and water at each other, feasting and using obscene language to drive away evil spirits.

On the *Phalguna Shukla* 15, the *Purva Phalguni nakshatra* appears. The deity of this *nakshatra* is *bhaga,* the female procreative organ. This explains the obscenities indulged in so freely during the Holi festival.

Holi is the legacy of ancient fertility rituals. Since ancient times, obscene dialogues, crude gestures, and even ritual intercourse have been a part of festivity along with singing, dancing and music. Abusive ritual dialogues with sexual overtones between a Brahmin and a harlot constituted an integral part of Vedic Mahavrata celebration. It was followed by intercourse between the harlot and Magadha. In the Vedic horse sacrifice, *ashvamedha,* the queen of the *yajna*-performing monarch sleeps with a horse and exchanges obscene dialogues with the priests.

In the *Kalika Purana,* there is a description of *Shavarotsava* which is celebrated on the tenth day of Durga Puja. The *Puranas* say that on that day, married and unmarried maidens as well as harlots dance to the accompaniment of musical instruments, such as the *shankha, turya, mridanga* and *pataha* while the people indulge in throwing mud and dust at each other and in uttering words, songs and actions about the female and male sex organs, *bhaga* and *linga.*

In ancient scriptures, we find mention of the ritual of hurling abuses and obscenities to please the deities. Devangana Desai in her work, *Erotic Sculpture of India,* points out:

> Jimutavahana, in the twelfth century, clearly states in his *Kalavilasa* that the goddess gets angry with the person who does not participate in actions, words and songs attributed to male and female sex organs.

In other words, obscenity during Holi has scriptural sanction as it is believed to enhance fertility, drive away the evil spirits and please the deities.

The early mention of Holi as *Phalgunotsava* is found in *Gatha Saptashati,* a collection of Maharashtri-Prakrit folk-verses by King Hala Satavahana and ascribed to the first or the second century AD. The *Gatha* says:

> Being perfectly legitimate during *Phalgunotsava,* your lover smears your lovely breasts with mud. But why are you trying to wash off this decoration with water again and again? The sweat caused by your lover's touch has already done that.

When exactly the name of Krishna, the lover of female cowherds, *gopis* got associated with this festival is not really known, but it certainly enhances the fun and frolic associated with it. For the first time it was in the *Garga Samhita,* a Puranic work written by Sage Garga on the life of Krishna that we find a very romantic description of Radha and Krishna playing Holi. Cowherd girls led by beautiful Radha sing the songs of Holi and abuse Krishna in jest while drenching him with coloured water.

The most boisterous Holi in entire India is celebrated in the Braj region where Krishna had spent his childhood days. It is a forty-day affair in the region where every village has its own tradition of celebrating the festival.

In Bengal and Orissa, Holi is celebrated as the *Dolotsava*, the swing festival of Krishna. Obscenities connected with Holi are generally confined to singing bawdy songs or uttering lewd words, at times accompanied by vulgar gestures but not by open display of phallic symbols. However, in north Karnataka, a straw puppet is made in the shape of a huge phallus that can be manipulated by a string. Such a puppet is known as *bittappa*. A long pole is pegged into the ground and the *bittappa* is suspended from the top.

Liquor, *Sura* is an ally of Kama. To make a girl shed her inhibitions and build up the erotic mood or feelings of *kama*, the *sura* was consumed. *Gohil Grihyasutra* prescribes the ritual of drenching the body of the bride at the time of her wedding by reciting the *mantra*: "Kama, I know thy name; intoxication is thy name."

Wine is freely consumed during Holi. In some Puranas, Kama is described as a chief of *Apsaras,* the great, heavenly beauties and seductresses, adept in dancing, singing and music. Performing arts naturally became part of Holi.

The ancient adoration of Kama and festivals associated with him like *Vasantotsava* has survived in the form of rituals and revelry of Holi, the festival of love and it's god, Kama!

Chapter Two

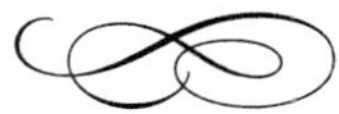

Business of Love

In ancient India, courtesans, *ganikas* conducted the business of love with élan. Apart from their trade interests, they were known for their active participation in social, cultural and even religious life of the people. Beautiful, intelligent, even learned, they were considered as a repository of arts and social graces. They constituted a part of literary gatherings, royal entourages, and at times, even military expeditions. They turned business into a fine art and entertainment industry.

Many courtesans are mentioned in literary works even by name. At the time of the Buddha, the most reputed *ganika* was Amrapali, famous as the *nagaravadhu* of Vaishali.

She was the daughter of Mahanam and many rich businessmen vied with each other to marry her due to her inherent beauty. Mahanam, in the assembly of *ganas,* declared his intention to give her in marriage to a suitable person, but the Gana Parishad decided that this gem of a woman should become *ganabhogya* or common property of all. Prior to accepting their decision to become *nagaravadhu,* Amrapali laid down certain conditions before them. These included the gift of a palatial mansion in the best part of the city of Vaishali, permission to charge a fee of five hundred gold coins per day, maintenance of her privacy when entertaining a customer, and freedom from surveillance by the state intelligence department. Her conditions were accepted.

Amrapali set up a large picture gallery in her mansion where she kept portraits of kings, rich men and traders. She was known to be adept in sixty-four arts and King Bimbisara was one of her lovers (*Sringarhat*, p. 68).

In the *Buddhacharita* of Ashvaghosha, Amrapali is described as one very proud of her beauty and youth. Once Buddha stayed in her pleasure garden at Vaishali. With great humility, Amrapali approached Tathagata and listened to his sermon. She donated her garden to the Buddhist Sangha and became a disciple of the Master.

In the *Therigatha*, a very ancient Buddhist work, her poetic and pathetic confession is found vividly recorded in a long piece of verse.

In the *Telapatta Jataka*, there is mention of a very famous *ganika* of the time by the name of *Janapadakalyani*. She was so adept in dancing and singing that thousands thronged to witness her performances. Extremely beautiful, she is described as being neither tall nor short, having a luscious body and golden complexion, teeth white and sparkling, and very graceful in her movements. Her very name suggests that she was one who belonged to the entire community, *ganabhogya*. Though she had attained the age of twenty, she looked like a sixteen-year old girl.

In the *Anabhirata Jataka*, it is said that by nature, a woman is available to all. A *Gatha* says:

> Wise men know that like the river, highway
> pub, gambling den, with water for the thirsty,
> a woman is by definition available for all.

Here, most probably, a veiled reference is made to public women or courtesans whose doors were open to all.

In the *Atthana Jataka*, we are told about the greedy nature of the *ganikas*. In the city of Varanasi, there lived a young son of a rich merchant named Mahadhanakumar. He fell in love with a beautiful *ganikas* of the city. Every night, he would pay her a thousand gold coins to make love to her. One day, due to some reason, he went to her without her fee of thousand gold coins. She immediately threw him out of her house, despite her long-standing association with him. The shocked and humiliated son of the merchant immediately left the city and became an ascetic. He took to living in a hut on the bank of river Ganga.

In the Buddhist work *Asokavadana*, considered to be written in the second century AD, there is the story of a very beautiful and young *ganika* of Mathura named Vasavadatta. Her fee per night was five hundred gold coins. The rich and mighty of the city courted her. In the same city, lived the handsome son of an incense-merchant whose name was Upagupta. The *ganika* Vasavadatta became infatuated with this young man, who was blessed with sterling qualities.

One day, she sent her attendant to Upagupta, inviting him to her mansion. Rejecting her advances politely, he said that time had not yet come to visit her. Vasavadatta presumed that probably he had been discouraged by the high rate of fee that she charged. She sent another message, saying, she did not demand any payment from him, but the young man repeated the same words in reply.

Shrugging off her lovely shoulders, she forgot about the handsome son of the merchant and as time passed, she continued leading her life of luxury. One day, when she was enjoying the company of a young son of a local merchant, she was informed about the arrival of another rich youth, loaded with numerous precious gifts, apart from her usual fee of five hundred gold coins.

The greedy *ganika*, in order to receive the more lucrative customer from a foreign land, got the local youth killed.

The crime of the courtesan was brought to the notice of the king. The infuriated king ordered her disfigurement and banishment from the town. At that time, the gentle son of the incense-merchant, Upagupta approached her and sat by her side with deep compassion reflecting in his kind eyes.

Smiling sadly, Vasavadatta said that when her body was like a beautiful lotus in full bloom, he did not visit her. "Do my disfigured lips covered with blood attract you, O young man?" she asked plaintively.

Upagupta nursed the wounds of Vasavadatta with utmost care till she died. The very next day of her death, Upagupta renounced the world and entered the order of Buddha. Later, he became the preceptor of Emperor Ashoka of Pataliputra.

Several interesting stories related to *ganikas* intersperse many of the literary works. Generally, they are depicted as parasites, greedy, hankering for money from their lovers to whom they show the door once they become penniless. Then, there are stories too about *ganika* who were very faithful even to their lovers despite their living in penury. There are also interesting stories of discarded lovers who took adequate revenge when insults were meted out to them.

Descriptions of the fabulous wealth accumulated by courtesans are found in many literary works. Even heads of religious sects were generous with them, according to *Kuttanimatam*. Pashupatacharya Bhavashuddha of Varanasi gifted the *ganika,* Anangadevi, a magnificent and opulent mansion, *dhavalagriha*, which became the talk of the entire town.

Brihatkatha is a collection of such stories in Paishachi language written by Gunadhya under the Satavahanas during the first or the second century AD. The original work was lost to posterity but its Sanskrit version entitled *Kathasaritsagara,* by Pandit Somadeva belonging to eleventh century, is still available. It contains a number of interesting stories about courtesans. The book mentions a beautiful *ganika* named Madanamala of Pratishthanpur, whose mansion was no less than the royal palace in its grandeur. Several flags fluttered on its top. Its eastern gate was guarded by twenty thousand foot-soldiers and the other gates by ten thousand soldiers each. The mansion had several horses and elephants in its stables apart from the seven ramparts, *prakaras*. Even kings took refuge in her mansion where customers were regaled with wine, dance and music.

There is an interesting story of a Brahmin who was well versed in the *Sama Veda* but was foolish by nature. Once he received a gift of eight grams of gold from a householder. He decided to visit the house of a *ganika* named Chaturika to acquire worldly wisdom that he lacked. He gave her the gold and requested her to be his guru. Everybody, assembled there, started laughing at him. To impress them, the foolish Vedic Brahmin started reciting the *Sama* hymns in a very high pitch. Troubled by his loud voice, the servants of the house threw him out. This proved to be his first lesson in worldly wisdom.

There is a humorous story of a rich son of a merchant called Ishvaradattta. During his business trip, he visited a city named Kanchanpur and in the evening he visited a temple, *devakula*, to witness an opera, *preshanaka*. There he saw a beautiful *ganika* Sundari, who was very adept in dancing. He spent all his money on her. When he lost everything, the *ganika's* mother Makarakati, threw him out of the house. Subsequently he was able to recover his wealth by tricking Sundari with the help of an old and experienced prostitute Kuttani Yamajivha, who was well trained in various postures of making love — *surate cha vidagdha*. Also in the same book, there is the story of a rich *ganika* of Ujjayani who lends her army to the defeated King Vikramasingh of Prathisthan, who was her lover and helps him recover his lost kingdom.

In the city of Mathura, there lived a beautiful *ganika* named Rupanika, whose mother Kuttani Makaradransta was very strict. One day, while Rupanika had gone to offer prayers at a temple, *surakula*, she saw a handsome young man, who happened to be a poor Brahmin named Lohajangha. She promptly fell in love with him and invited him to her mansion where they revelled in love-making. So infatuated was she with the Brahmin lad that she stopped entertaining her other customers. This infuriated her old Kuttani mother, who with the help of her armed guards, drove him out of her house. The story continues to tell how Lohajangha returns and takes his revenge.

In the fourth century BC, Bhasa, one of the earliest Sanskrit dramatists, wrote a play *Charudattam*, based on the love-story of a Brahmin, who is a merchant by profession, and of a beautiful *ganika* named Vasantasena. Shudraka in the fifth to the sixth century AD, wrote its extended version under the title *Mricchakatika,* which became very famous. The play gives us insight into the lifestyles of the courtesan class, *ganika*.

While describing the ambience of the house of *ganika* Vasantasena, Bhasa says that scholars of different traditional sciences, *Agamas* and *Nagamas*, visited her from different cities to read books in her house and held discussions with her. This indicates the intellectual level of the ancient *ganikas*. However, it was Shudraka, who described in elaborate detail the various parts of the huge mansion in which Vasantasena lived and the different activities that took place therein.

In the amazing world of Vasantasena, a library was maintained so that the clients could read books. Young girls aspiring to be *ganikas* were adequately trained in vocal and instrumental music, dancing, singing and enactment of erotic dramas — *natyam sasringaram*. The rich merchants were treated with fine wine, rich food and gambling boards for their entertainment. Vasantasena's mansion was no less than heaven where *apsaras*, bedecked with fine jewellery made of gold and precious stones moved around to entertain their guests.

Despite all this luxury, Shudraka does not deter from describing the ill effects of excessive drinking of liquor like *sidhu*, *sura* and *asava* on the inmates of these abodes of pleasure. Vasantasena, says Shudraka, was as beautiful as *Vasanta ritu* itself — *vasantashobheva Vasantasena*. She was an expert in the theatrical arts and knew how to modulate her voice — *rangapraveshena kalanam chaiva shikshaya, swarantarena daksha*. This rich *ganika* of Ujjayani loved a poverty-ridden but handsome Brahmin youth and remained steadfast in her love for him during a period when faithfulness was considered a rare quality in a *ganika*.

Kuttanimatam gives a long list of such *ganikas*. It mentions *ganikas* who went to the extent of committing self-immolation, *sati* on the funeral pyre of their dead lovers. It speaks of a rich *ganika* of Varanasi who donated all her well-earned wealth to her lover Nilakantha, whom she adored intensely. Stricken with love, another *ganika* Kadambaka forsook her luxurious lifestyle to go and live with her poor lover, Bhatta Vishnu, who was the son of Jihalla Mishra.

We have already seen that the *Acharya* of Pashupata sect gifted a magnificent palace, *dhavalagriha*, for the *ganika* he loved. *Ganikas* had a soft corner for religious gurus. *Kuttanimatam* says that when the Jain guru, Nagnacharya Narasimha, entered the fire, the *ganika* who loved him dearly followed suit.

The *ganikas* followed different religious sects. Amrapali became a Buddhist and so did Vasantasena. Some *ganikas* were followers of Jainism. An interesting inscription from Mathura, belonging to as early as first century BC, says:

> Adoration for Arhat Vardhamana, the daughter of the matron courtesan Lonasobhika, a disciple of the ascetics, the junior courtesan Vasu erected a shrine dedicated to Arhat; it had a hall of homage (*ayagasabha*), a cistern (and) a stone slab at the sanctuary of Nirgrantha Arhata, of her mother, her sister, her daughter, her son and her whole household, in honour of Arhata (*Miracle Plays of Mathura*, p. 252).

In the Jina work *Vasudevahindi* we meet a *ganika* named Kamapadaga, who vows to observe an eight-day festival, *attahiya*, in honour of the Jinas. However, in ancient India, courtesans generally worshipped the Vedic deity, Kamadeva, whose temple formed a part of the locality in which they resided.

Bhana plays were part of the life of the *ganikas*. Particularly famous are four plays — *Padmaprabhisaritaka* by Shudraka, *Dhurtavitasamvada* by Ishvaradatta, *Ubhayabhisarika* by Vararuchi and *Padataditaka* by Shyamilaka. They are purported to have been written sometime between the end of fourth and the beginning of fifth century AD. The plays are full of humour, wit, sarcasm, and even obscenity. These playful satires when grouped together are known as *Chaturbhani*. A critic writing in the centenary supplement of *Journal of Royal Asiatic Society*, 1924, about these plays, says:

> It will, I think, be admitted that these compositions, in spite of the unedifying character of their general subject and even in spite of the occasional vulgarities, have a real literary quality. They display natural humour and a polite, intensely Indian, irony which need not fear

comparison with a Ben Jonson or a Moliere. The language is the veritable ambrosia of Sanskrit speech (p. 135).

People from all strata of society, including the ascetics, monks and Vaishnavas, visited the *vesha*. In the *Padmaprabhrutakam*, we come across a Shakya *bhikshu* named Sanhilaka who, while moving in the *vesha*, is shown concealing his identity by covering himself with a long piece of white cloth. Vita, a vagabond parasite haunting the location of *ganikas*, calls him a ghost from the Buddhist monastery, *vihar vetal*. On being caught, he pompously says that he was in the *vesha* to console Sanghadasika, a *ganika,* who was feeling disturbed over the death of her mother and that it was his religious duty to show compassion to all living beings. However Vita exposes his real intention, which, according to him, was to indulge in love-making with *ganikas* and drink wine. The monk beats a hasty retreat.

In the *Ubhayabhisarika* of Vararuchi, we meet the beautiful, religious mendicant, Parivrajika Vilaskaundini, belonging to the Kanad philosophy of Vaisheshika *darshan*. Vita accuses her of enjoying love-making with her lover despite her being an ascetic. With her witty retort, she renders him speechless.

Hypocrisy of Pavitraka, son of Dharmasanik, who calls himself a Vaishnava, is exposed in the play *Padmaprabhrutakam* by Vita. In the same play, we encounter the Brahmin youth, Shaishilaka. In her neighbourhood lives a Buddhist nun, *shakyabhikshyaki*. On getting overwhelmed by passion, Malatika, a daughter of a garland-maker, sends a nun, to Shaishilaka as her messenger, or *duti*. Instead of going to Malatika, he perforce makes love to the nun.

It was a common practice in those days to employ nuns and female ascetics to carry love messages because of their easy accessibility. It was very easy for them to reach the womenfolk of the house and deliver the messages of their paramours.

Ganikas were trained as actresses. Among the well-known sixty-four arts they were expected to learn, many were related to the dramatic arts. Chaturbhani provides us with evidence of their participation in dramatic performances. In *Ubhayabhisarika*, there is a reference to a *ganika*, Madanasena who performs a musical named *Madanaradhana* in the temple of Bhagavan Narayana Vishnu of Pataliputra. In the same *bhana*, the *ganika*, Priyangusena, tells Vita that she has received an invitation to perform a musical entitled *Purandaravijaya* in the palace of Emperor Kumaragupta along with the *ganika* named Devdatta.

In the *Kuttanimatam*, there is an elaborate description of the enactment of the first act in Harsha's play *Ratnavali* by the *ganikas* of Varanasi in the Kashi Vishwanatha temple. However, Nrityachaya, the director of the play, is very caustic in his remarks about *ganikas* acting in dramatic performances. He says:

> How can there be excellence in stage shows when wicked and deceitful prostitutes act in them? Some are dominated by overpowering lovers, some do not leave for a moment the customer of their choice and some do not budge from the door of their house with the hope that anytime a rich customer may arrive. When a prostitute acting on the stage learns that an acquaintance has arrived at her house, she at once leaves the stage and rushes home. Without a sense of dedication, there cannot be good acting. And one cannot expect that from a courtesan who is engrossed in drinking wine, eating non-vegetarian food and making love to men. At times, these not-very-enthusiastic courtesans, fearing a loss of their source of income, do move their hands and legs in the name of play-acting but their minds are elsewhere.

Kuttanimatam is a unique work by Damodaragupta who served the ruler of Kashmir, King Jayapida in the eighth century AD. It elaborately describes the deceitful and fraudulent ways of *ganikas*, their mothers, their pimps like Vitas and Kuttanis, and how men fell prey to them and lost their wealth. The basic intention was to caution the men and save them from falling prey to women of easy virtue.

As *ganikas* took to play-acting, womenfolk belonging to the acting community took to prostitution. A woman most desirable for making love is an actress who has just returned to back stage after her performance — *rangottirna nati* — says a Prakrit verse included in the *Gatha Saptashati*.

It is obvious from the remark that Sita makes in the *Ramayana* when Rama comes to take leave from her before going to exile. She angrily says:

> Like an actor, Rama wants me to give in to others — *shailusha evamam Rama parebhyo datumicchasi.*

Vatsyayana, in his *Kamasutra*, has included *nati* (*Rangayoshit*) Yashodhara in the list of courtesans belonging to different categories.

A *nata* was called a *jayajiva*, one who lived by the income of his wife. *Manusmriti* says wives of Charanas lived through prostitution. Patanjali, who is considered as one of the great classical writers on Hindu scriptures, in his *Mahabhashya* says:

> When the womenfolk of *natas* (actresses) arrive on the stage, members of the audience shout 'To whom do you belong, to whom do you really belong' and they reply, 'To you, to you.'

In the Buddhist work *Avadanashataka*, there is an interesting story about a dancer-cum-actress Kuvalaya, who is the charming and lovely daughter of a drama director from south, *natacharya* of *dakshinapatha*. The *natacharya* happens to be on a visit to Rajgriha to attend the festival known as *Girivalgusamagama*. Kuvalaya is very beautiful and proud of her shapely body bursting with youth. Spectators hold their breath in wonderment on seeing her perform on the stage.

On learning of the reputation of the Buddha, she approaches him after bedecking herself in a beautiful dress and all her fine jewellery. She then performs a most provocative dance, baring her attractive body — *nrutyati gayati vadayate streelingani streechinhani, streenimittani chopadarshayati.* The monks get distraught at such blatant display of her physical assets. For performing this nude dance, she invites the wrath of Tathagata who curses her.

Perhaps, dancers in ancient India did not mind exposing their lovely bodies. The metal figurine of a dancer excavated at Mohenjodaro and ascribed to 2500 BC is frankly nude. In the *Rig Veda,* the goddess of morn Usha, is compared to a dancer who bares her lovely bosom.

In the *Mahabharata*, there is a story of Sage Vishvamitra and an *apsara,* Menaka. When she wanted to seduce the sage and test his steadfastness, she moved before him in the nude.

The greatest poet-dramatist of India, Kalidasa, who belonged to the fifth century AD and wrote three plays — *Abhijnana Shakuntala, Malavikagnimitra* and *Vikramorvashiya*, all of which were based on love. In poet Kalidasa's play *Malavikagnimitra*, the heroine Malavika is asked to appear *vigatanepathya* for her dance performance so that the beauty of her entire body is visible. *Sarvanga sausthava abhivyakti* — here *vigatanepathya* may mean 'in the nude' or 'in the skimpiest possible costume,' which is fully revealing.

In the Buddhist *Nalinika Jataka*, we see Princess Nalinika exposing her body while playing with a ball in full view of a young sage, Rishi Sringa, who has not seen a woman before, in order to seduce him. The legend is that Rishi Sringa, who was born from the union of a sage and a beautiful *apsara,* had been so protected by his father that he had never set his eyes on any one other than his father and hence had no idea what a woman looked like.

According to *Prabandhachintamani*, King Paramardin of Kuntal witnesses a nude female dancer give a dance performance in his court.

Ganikas from different foreign lands adorned the *veshas* of India since ancient times. In Mahakavi Shyamilaka's *bhana, Padataditaka*, there is an interesting description of a Greek, *Yavana ganika* whose words are incomprehensible to the local people of Ujjayani. The fair, charming *ganika's* name is given as Karpuraturistha, meaning 'fair as camphor'. The *bhana* says:

> And who is this girl? O, she is none other than *yavani* Karpuraturistha, beloved of my dear friend and Shardulavarma's son, Varahadas.
>
> Holding with three fingers, she raises the cup of wine to the moon. On her cheeks are reflected shining moon-shaped ear-rings that she tries to push back with her other hand. The light from her beautiful rings falls on her smooth shoulders in an arc, appearing as though the moon itself rests on her shoulders.
>
> The beautiful *yavini* with eyes like that of a *chakora* (bird's) eyes is

> pushing back her hair by the nails of her slender fingers while looking at the reflection of her face in the goblet full of wine. Her *madhuka* (flower) -like fair and delicate cheeks become pink due to the drinking of wine. Thinking it to be rouge, she, in vain trying to rub it off.
>
> I know her, but no, I will not dare to speak with her. Who would like to listen to her speech full of unfamiliar consonants which she utters like a shrieking monkey, trying to explain its meaning by gesticulation?

Probably she was not the only foreign girl in the *vesha* of Ujjayani because Vita says that the words uttered by *ganikas* and *yavanis* were virtually synonymous.

Helen, the wife of Emperor Chandragupta Maurya (fourth century BC), was Greek in origin. She was the daughter of Seleucus Nicator who ruled over some parts of north-west India after Alexander left the region.

Foreign girls were in demand in India since ancient times. Early records reveal that 'singing girls' or 'flute girls' were exported to India by enterprising slave-traders. In the first century AD, a book entitled *Periplus of the Erythrean Sea* was written. It is described as the "only ancient mariner's manual on the coasts of India that is still in existence." It lists among popular Greek merchandise coming to India, the singing boys and beautiful maidens as also costly silverware and fine wine.

In the second act of Kalidasa's play *Abhijnana Shakuntala*, King Dushyanta is shown entering the stage, surrounded by female *yavani* guards, wearing garlands of flowers and carrying bows and arrows in their hands. Kalidasa lived in Ujjayani and wrote his plays around the fourth to fifth century AD. The reference to *yavanis* in his play indicates that during the Gupta period, Greek girls indeed lived in Ujjayani.

In ancient India, courtesans, *ganikas,* played a major role in the social and cultural life of the people. In the *Kamasutra* it is recorded that any citizen, *nagaraka*, should convene a social gathering, *goshthi,* at the house of a *ganika* to discuss arts and literature. The commentator Yashodhara says that he should hold discussions on poetic works such as the *Mahabharata* and arts, including dancing — *bharatadikavyasya nrityadikalaya va charchasyat*. He is also advised to go on picnics along with *ganikas*.

The elders believed that feelings of love soar with wine. The fragrance of flowers and the choicest of liquors made the ambience of the *vesha* enticing and alluring. It was considered that wines stimulate sexual passion and enhance the pleasure of love-making.

Wine drinking was prevalent in ancient times as depicted in epics and the *Puranas*. Even the women of royal families drank wine.

It was poet Kalidasa who introduced the cult of wine on to the Indian stage. He was the first to include bacchanalian scenes in his five act play *Malavikagnimitra*. Here we see Iravati, the young and beautiful wife of King Agnimitra, appearing on the stage in a fully drunken state. On her entry, an interesting conversation takes place between Iravati and her maid-servant, Nipunika.

> *Iravati*: O Nipunika, I have heard that after drinking wine women start looking more beautiful. Is there any truth in this saying?
> *Nipunika*: When I look at you, it seems to be quite true.

The tradition of introducing bacchanalian scenes on the stage was continued by Sriharsha. In his play *Ratnavali*, we see inebriated *ganikas* dancing and singing to celebrate the spring festival.

Ganikas were very fond of wine as a stimulant. In the *bhana* play, *Dhurtavitasamvada* by Isvaradatta, there is an interesting reference to a cup of wine in the shape of a dancing peacock.

It was considered romantic to sit close to a *ganika* or share a single seat with her, *ardhasana*, and drink wine. In the Ajanta cave paintings, such types of drinking scenes are found painted in abundance.

At the National Museum in New Delhi, there is an interesting sculpture showing a man and his beloved, most probably a courtesan, sitting close to each other in the *ardhasana* posture with the man holding a cup of wine. Women are shown dancing in front of them.

There is a large sculptural panel in the National Museum showing a drunken courtesan lifted up by her lover. On the reverse is a scene from the play *Mricchakatika* wherein the courtesan Vasantasena is being pursued by Vita and Shakara.

However, the most charming sculpture showing a courtesan drinking wine in a standing posture has been found at Sanghol in Punjab. Here a nude girl is shown emptying the glass of wine held to her lips in the bottoms-up position. With her eyes half closed, her face looks flushed after consuming wine.

Carved in relief on the uprights of railings are very beautiful female figures that were found in Mathura. They are ascribed to the Kushana period. These sensuous figures in different attitudes seem to have been inspired by the courtesans of the city. At Pal Khera, a foreign courtesan is shown serving wine to a pot-bellied man.

From *bhana* play, *Padataditaka*, we learn that paths leading to the *vesha* were lined with wine or liquor shops, *panagara*, where people would get drunk. The gamblers, who had won some money in gambling, are shown moving towards the *vesha* with wine bottles in their hands, obviously to enjoy their drinks in the company of courtesans of their choice.

Apart from four *bhana* plays of the Gupta period, we find a number of *bhana* plays written subsequently with *vesha* and courtesans constituting their main themes.

Another form of drama, *prahasana*, means 'satire'. Some famous comical plays are *Latakamelakam* written by Shankhadhar in the twelfth century, *Dhurtasamagama* written by Jyotirishvar Kavishekhar in the fifteenth century and *Hasyarnava* of Jagadishvara belonging to the same period. In addition to the above-mentioned, *Dhurtanartak* by Samaraj Dikshit, *Kautukaratnakara* by Laxman Manikyadeva, *Sringarabhushana* by Vamana Bhatta Bana, *Sringaratilaka* by Ramachandra Dikshit, *Vasantatilaka* by Varadacharya, and *Sringarasarvasva* by Nalla Kavi are some other well-known comical plays. While describing the lives of *ganikas*, these farces tend to become obscene rather than humorous.

Another interesting poetic work depicting the *vesha* culture in six hundred and forty-five verses is *Samayamatrika,* written by

Kshemendra in AD 1050. It is in the same class as *Kuttanimatam*, which has been mentioned earlier. Nearly in all the books on *Kamashastra*, the *ganikas* are described.

The best-known farce, *prahasana,* on the theme is *Bhagavadajjukiyam* by Boudhayana. It is known for its subtle sense of humour and high literary standard. The farce is based on a piquant situation. Due to a mistake committed by *Yamaduta*, the agent of god of death, the souls of a *ganika* and an ascetic get exchanged and all hell breaks loose. The ascetic starts behaving as a *ganika* and the *ganika* as an ascetic. Ultimately, *Yamaduta* rectifies his mistake and both go their individual ways. This situation-based farce is unique in the entire genre of Sanskrit drama.

According to Indian tradition, the first author to write on *veshiki* or the topic related to *vesha* was Dattaka. Vatsyayana in his *Kamasutra* says that Dattaka wrote this work on the request of the courtesans of Pataliputra. His work, *Dattakasutra*, written in the first or second century AD, has been lost to posterity. In the *bhana* plays, *Dhurtavitasamvada* and *Padataditaka*, the *sutras* of Dattaka are quoted. Writing about him in his commentary on *Kamasutra*, Yashodhara says that Dattaka is the son of a Mathur Brahmin of Pataliputra. His mother died after giving birth to him. His father gave him to another Brahmin and left the city. Dattaka learnt the various arts and sciences, *kala* and *vidya,* and became famous as Dattakacharya. He acquired worldly wisdom, *lokayatra*, from the *ganikas*. The *ganikas*, led by Virasena, requested him to write a treatise on *veshiki* and so he wrote *Dattakasutra*.

The history of prostitution dates back to several centuries. Vedic literature testifies to it. In the *Smritis* too, the prostitutes are mentioned. In the *Arthashastra* of Kautilya, a special chapter is devoted to *ganikadhyakshya prakarana*, which among other things explains the relationship between state administration and courtesans.

It is said that it was Sage Dirghatamas who laid down the rule of paying a woman for making love to her and that probably led to the institution of prostitution.

The name of Rishi Dirghatamas is mentioned in the *Rig Veda.* A number of legends about him are found in the *Mahabharata* and the *Puranas.* He was blind by birth but well versed in Vedic lore and sciences (*shastras*). He married a lovely, young woman named Pradweshi. From the sons of Kamadhenu, the divine cow, he learnt *gorati vidya* or knowledge on the ways of the bull and which he put into practice while performing sexual intercourse with the cow. However, some scholars translate *gorati* as public copulation. Interestingly, in the *Kamasutra* of Vatsyayana, bovine sexual postures such as *dhenuka* and *goyuthika* are mentioned.

When Dirghatamas started copulating in the open like a bull, with a cow, the other sages in the hermitage decided to throw him out. Bored with the old man, his wife too backed the decision of the sages. She wanted to marry someone young instead.

An angry Dirghatamas laid down certain laws for women. He said:

> One husband is for a woman the first thing and the last so long as she is alive. Whether he be dead or alive, she shall have no other man. But if a wife goes to another man, then unfailingly she sinks out her caste. And for an unwedded woman, too, it is from today a crime leading to loss of caste. But if copulation does come about, then all men must give her money; the women withal are not to have any profit from the pleasure, but it shall ever be dishonour and shame for them. (Meyer)

Angered by this, Pradweshi and her sons bound the blind, old man to a raft and dumped him in river Ganga.

Dirghatamas floated down the river but the rules he had laid down continue to exist and since then, people began to pay money to women for the sexual favours granted to men. And, here, some scholars think, lies the origin of prostitution.

The traits of a *ganika* are seen in the character of *apsara* Urvashi of the *Rig Veda.* In this *Veda,* we find a hymn in the form of a dialogue between King Pururava and Urvashi. Urvashi, fiercely independent and self-willed, deserts her lover Pururava, as a *ganika* probably would to retain her freedom. When he tries to unite with her again, she bluntly rebuffs him by saying that the bond of loyalty does not exist and that their hearts are the hearts of jackals. In the *Shatapatha Brahmana*, the *apsaras* are described as engaged in dance, song, and play. In later mythology, they indeed were considered as *ganikas* of heaven.

Ganikas were present in all ages. Their presence was felt prominently for the first time in the *Mahabharata*. In the ancient Buddhist and Jain texts, we find the names of famous *ganikas* of the time. It is obvious from the *Chaturbhani* that the profession flourished and became a virtually complete entertainment industry. Plays were written on the lives of *ganikas*, prominent among them being *Mricchakatika* of Shudraka. Independent works like *Kuttanimatam* and *Samayamatrika* describing the *vesha* culture were written in the eighth and eleventh centuries respectively. The profession continued to flourish in the Middle Ages too.

Chapter Three

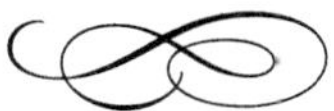

Learning of Love

The ancients committed knowledge of love to books, treatises and manuals from which one can learn the art of love-making. The *Vedas* emphasise upon the primacy of sexual instinct by stating that it was Kama who was born first and will forever be great. The Vedic people practised the art of seduction, occasionally by frankly describing the sexual act and saying,

> A woman is a sacrifical fire, her procreative organ is a fire-altar and coital bliss is the spark.

They went to the extent of stating that the procreative organ, *upastha,* is the one and only source of bliss. Ignorance in the science of making love was deprecated and the procedure of how to approach the wife to beget the desired progeny was laid down.

But we do not know if the Vedic people wrote any independent treatise on the art of love-making as such. Even if they had written one, it is lost to posterity.

However, Vatsyayana in his *Kamasutra,* has traced the history of *kamashastric* literature. He says:

> Prajapati, the lord of creation, pronounced the science covering three basic aspects of human life — *dharma, artha* and *kama* — in one lakh chapters. In that he laid down rules to regulate human existence. *Dharma* is duty, acquisition of religious merit; *artha* is acquisition of wealth and property; and *kama* is enjoyment of sexual pleasure and gratification of senses.

It was a voluminous work and hence Swayambhuva Manu separated the portion related to *dharma*, Brihaspati related to *artha* and Nandi, related to *kama*. Each of these works contained one thousand chapters. Nandi is described as an attendant to Mahadeva. Yashodhara, in his Jayamangala commentary on *Kamasutra,* says that Nandi, who stood at the gate of Shiva's *vasagriha,* watched for one thousand years his master's indulgence in sexual pleasures with his consort Parvati and subsequently created his *Kamashastra* in a thousand chapters. This was quite voluminous.

Nandi's *Kamasutra* was condensed into five hundred chapters by Swetaketu, son of Uddalaka Aruni.

As a great *acharya* and Vedic scholar, Uddalaka Aruni is frequently mentioned in the *Upanishads* as also in the *Mahabharata*. He belonged to the Gautama clan and was a resident of Panchala country. Swetaketu, his son, was equally proficient in Vedic lore and *yajna karma*.

According to *Brihadaranyaka Upanishada,* Swetaketu once went to the court of Pravahana Jival, king of Panchala country and received instructions from him. It seems that Pravahana initiated Swetaketu in the mysteries of sexual relationships. He told him that a woman is fire, her procreative organ is firewood, pubic hair is the snake, *yoni* is flame, intercourse is ember and sexual pleasure is spark. The *Upanishad* contains a full chapter on the procedure of procreation and how to beget a desired progeny. It records the opinions of Uddalak Aruni and two other sages, Nakamaudgalya and Kumaraharita, that many Brahmins indulged in the sexual act without properly knowing the science of love-making, *maithuna vigyan* and thus suffer ignominy. It also speaks of birth-control methods and how to vanquish the paramour of one's wife by use of black magic.

According to the *Mahabharata*, Swetaketu and his father Uddalaka Aruni were responsible for laying down the foundation of the institution of marriage. According to a legend, a Brahmin asked Uddalaka Aruni to lend him his wife for procreating a son as per the custom prevalent then.

Swetaketu laid down the rule that a woman should have only one husband.

According to the Jayamangala commentary on Vatsyayana's *Kamasutra*, Swetaketu tried to establish a new social code. He advised the Brahmins to desist from drinking liquor or sexually enjoying another man's wife. In his *Kamasutra*, Vatsyayana has quoted at least thrice the opinions expressed by Swetaketu.

Swetaketu's work too was quite bulky. It was further condensed into one hundred and fifty chapters by Babhravya (son of Babhru) of Panchala country. He reproduced the work in seven chapters which were as follows:

Sadharana — general sexology;
Samprayogic — sexual union;
Kanyasamprayuktaka — seduction of virgins;
Bharyadhikarik — pleasing the wives;
Paradarik — seducing the woman;
Veshik — about courtesans and
Aupanishadik — aphrodisiacs, herbs, love charms, etc.

All these topics are dealt separately by Charayana, Suvarnanabha, Ghotakamukha, Gonardia, Gonikaputra, Dattaka and Kuchumara.

The *Kamasutra* says that at the request of the *ganikas* of Pataliputra led by Virasena, Dattaka wrote a treatise on *veshika*. Thus, Babhravya's work was divided into a number of treatises, which made them lose their comprehensiveness. Vatsyayana went back to Babhravya's extensive work and abridged it, covering all the topics.

This brings us to the inevitable question : who was Vatsyayana?

We know practically nothing about Vatsyayana except that his name was Mallanaga *gotra*. He belonged to the Vatsyayana *gotra* or sect. In the concluding chapter of his work, he says that by collecting the works of experts on the subject of the past, by studying them and observing men and women indulging in the sexual act very carefully, he has written his book. While remaining celibate and after deep contemplation, he wrote the treatise.

Vatsyayana mentions King Kuntyala Satakarni Satavahana of Prathisthan and who belonged to the opening years of first century AD. K.M. Panikkar points out that in Subandhu's *Vasavadatta* written in fifth century AD, there is a passage that mentions the *Kamasutra* by name:

> It (the mountain which the poet was describing) was filled with elephants and was fragrant with perfumes of its jungles just as the *Kamasutra* written by Mallanaga contains the delight and enjoyment of a mistress.

He also refers to the Cambodian inscription of Yaco Varman (AD 889-900) carrying the following verse:

> Experts in the art of love, as if they have been taught by Vatsyayana and others.

This means that we can say that Vatsyayana was present between the first and fifth century AD. Scholars prefer to place him in the third century AD, or may be a century earlier.

Vatsyayana was a very realistic person who fully knew the limitations of the sex manual he had written instructing how to kiss, embrace, or make love in different postures. He has written at the end of the chapter on embrace that once the wheel of passion is set in motion, one can remember no orderly procedure or *shastra* — *ratichakre pravritte tu naiva shastram nacha kramah* (2.2.31).

Kamasutra is a veritable encyclopaedia of the contemporary social and cultural life. It has deeply influenced Indian literature and the arts.

In his work, *A South Indian Treatise on Kamasutra*, Swami Shivapriyananda writes:

> There are six commentaries on the *Kamasutra* of which the *Jayamangala* of Yashodhara is the most comprehensive and well-known. This commentary was written under the patronage of Chahamana king, Visaladeva (AD 1153-1163). The celebrated scholar, Kshemendra, student of great Abhinavagupta and court-poet of King Ananta of Kashmir (AD 1029-1064) is said to have written a summary on Vatsyayana's work appropriately called *Vatsyayana Sutra Sara* (Essence of Vatsyayana's Sutras). This commentary, however, is lost. The commentary by Virabhadradeva is well known as an independent work called *Kandarpacudamani* (Tiara of God of Love). This is a very skilful and faithful reworking in Aryan metre, of the entire *Kamasutra*, and was probably ghost-written by a court-scholar for King Virabhadradeva (AD 1577), son of Ramachandradeva of the Vaghela

dynasty of western India. There are two minor and less known commentaries — one is by Malladeva and the other is anonymous. A late commentary by Bhaskara Narasimha was written sometime at the end of the eighteenth century and is known as the *Vatsyayana Sutra Vritti*.

A very fascinating, but unfortunately lost, work on erotica was the remarkable *Gunapataka* (Standard of Good Qualities) by the notorious figure, generally known to later Sanskrit literature as Muladeva, though he had many aliases such as Mulabhadra, Bhadra, Devadatta and Karnisuta. The last name suggests that his mother's name was Karni, but his father's name is not known. He was a master in the dubious craft of pilfering and adept in the art of enticing young women. He was the very personification of chicanery. Crooks, cheats, scoundrels, vagabonds and all types of villainous characters surrounded him day and night. He gave them all good advice and guidance and at night, he sat on a high pedestal to give well-attended discourses on how to cheat, defraud, swindle and steal their favourite criminal subjects. He is said to have amassed a sizeable fortune with the help of his special associates Vipula, Achala, Shashi and Kandali.

Muladeva was so charismatic that many young men wanted to be his students and acolytes. Kshemendra in his *Kalavilasa* says that a wealthy merchant called Hiranyagupta placed his son Chandragupta in Muladeva's care to be trained and educated in the art of cheating. Like all gangsters, Muladeva loved women and two famous courtesans, Devadatta and Anangasena, who fought bitterly for his attention. But Muladeva admired the more experienced courtesan named Gunapataka and is said to have composed his work with the same name to immortalise her. Though the *Gunapataka* text is not available to us today, it was probably written in a form of a dialogue between the author and his beloved courtesan, Gunapataka. Muladeva's date is not known for certain, but Dandin, the author of the classical Sanskrit prose-romance *Dashakumaracharita*, mentions him by name Karnisuya — he lived before the sixth century AD (pp. 13-14).

In *Padmaprabhrutaka*, the *bhana* play of early Gupta period, by Shudraka, we find Karniputra and his love affairs mentioned. He is said to have been in love with the elder *ganika*, Devadatta, and her teenaged sister, Devasena. He lived in the city of Ujjayani. In the play, he is described as one coming from a good family, is intelligent and speaks with a smile on his lips, is clever and without malice towards anybody. He is said to be young, possessing many qualities and good looks; in other words, he is Kamadeva himself but without his bow. Probably he was the author of *Kamasutra Prakarana* — the book that, according to the *bhana* play, aroused the passion of his teenaged beloved, Devasena.

Sometime between the eighth and thirteenth centuries, Padmashri wrote a *kamashastric* work, known as *Nagarasarvasva*. We know nothing about the author. In the opening benedictory verse, he equates Smara or Kamadeva carrying the arrows of flowers with Arya Manjusri, a Buddhist deity. The book betrays the influence of Buddhist religion. For instance, in order to beget good progeny, stress is laid on the worship of Tara, a Buddhist deity. Hence, some scholars presume Padmashri to be a Buddhist monk.

In the early seventh century, the Pallava king of Kanchi, Mahendra Vikrama Varman, wrote a hilarious play, entitled *Mattavilas Prahasana*. In this play a Buddhist monk, who is a Shakya *bhikshu*, revels in his soliloquy:

> Compassionate Lord Buddha allowed us monks to reside in palaces, sleep on cosy beds, relish food in the first part of the day, drink sweet fruit juices in the afternoon, eat fragrant betel leaf and wear silk robes. And pray, do you think he would have prohibited the *bhikshus* from enjoying the company of women and drinking of wine? Certainly the old *bhikshus*, out of jealousy, must have removed the relevant passages from the *Pitaka,* book of law of conduct. So, why should I not endeavour to find out untampered original work and preach the tenets of Buddhism in their entirety and oblige the Sangha, the community of monks?

The Sangha had cordial relations with *ganikas*. The famous *ganika* Amrapali, known as the *nagarvadhu* of Vaishali, not only made generous contributions to the Sangha, she even became a disciple of the order. Vasantasena, the famous heroine of Shudraka's immortal play *Mricchakatika*, seems to have converted to Buddhism. In the *bhana* play *Padataditaka* by Mahakavi Shyamilaka, we find the caricature of a Buddhist monk who was seen moving secretly in the locality of courtesans.

Vatsyayana, in his *Kamasutra*, points to the prevailing practice of utilising the sevices of female ascetics and Buddhist nuns to procure women.

In the play *Malati Madhava* by Bhavabhuti, we see the Buddhist nun, Kamandaki, acting as a procuress or go-between the two lovers, Malati and Madhava. In Kalidasa's play, *Malavikagnimitra*, there is the female ascetic who is addressed as *Parivrajika Pandita Kaushiki* and who is described as a female procuress, *pithamardika*.

Under the circumstances, one should not be surprised at a Buddhist monk writing a *kamashastric* work. Moreover, the emergence of *tantric* Buddhism and its branches, such as Vajrayana and Sahajayana, led to sexo-yogic practices and enjoyment of one's senses, leading to sexual bliss, *mahasukha*. This must have liberated the *bhikshus* from the orthodox view of life which shunned sexual pleasures as is evident from the soliloquy of the Buddhist monk in the play, *Mattavilas Prahasana*.

The play, *Ananga Ranga* (Theatre of Love) was composed by Kalyana Malla, who belonged to the royal family of King Trilokchandra of Chandravamsha. Kalyana Malla was a son borne by Gajmalla to Trilokchandra. Kalyana Malla describes himself as a *mahakavi*, an expert in sixty-four acts and as *bhupamuni* or *rajarshri*.

He wrote the *Ananga Ranga* for Lad Khan of Lodi dynasty, who was the son of Ahmad Badshah. There is a lot of speculation on who Lad Khan was. The ancestors of Kalyana Malla too are not known to history. But the work became very famous and popular. Swami Shivapriyananda informs us that it has been translated into Arabic, Persian and Turkish languages and is known as *Lizzat-ul-Nissa*. The book was probably written at the close of fifteenth century AD.

There are a number of minor *kamashastric* works, such as *Panchasayaka* by Jyotirishvara Kavishekhara of fourteenth century, *Ratirahasya Pradipa* by Maharaja Devraja of seventeenth century and *Kandarpachudamani* by King Virabhadra of Vaghela dynasty of sixteenth century.

Probably more works were written on the subject over the centuries but which were either lost or are in manuscript form waiting to be noticed.

Quite recently Swami Sivapriyananda edited and published the *Ratì Ratna Pradipika* by Praudha Devaraja Maharaja of Wodeyar, the royal family of Mysore belonging to the seventeenth century AD. This text, for the purpose of publication, is beautifully illustrated by a contemporary artist, 'Ganjifa' Raghupati Bhatta, who is known for his erotic *(ganjifa)* paintings on playing cards.

Chapter Four

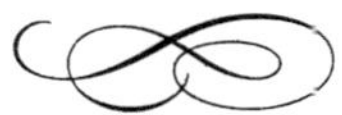

Rituals of Love

Love reached religion via sex rituals. The first great Indian civilisation known to history is the Indus Valley civilisation that flourished between 3500-1500 BC. We know very little about the religion of the Indus people, their practices or rituals. A large collection of terracotta figurines of nude Mother Goddesses have been excavated at different sites as also ring stones and phallic stones. On one seal, found at Mohenjodaro is depicted a three-headed ithyphallic deity sitting in *yogic* posture, surrounded by animals. He is described as the "earliest recognisable representation of divinity in human form in Indian art." On yet another seal, female figurines with horns are seen entwined around trees and are symbols of fertility or tree-spirits. Evidences from a later period reveal that a strong sexual element prevailed in the cult of Mother Goddess, the fertility spirit and the ithyphallic Shiva.

Some of the rituals of Vedic Aryans were permeated with sexual symbolisms or sexual acts themselves in either a subdued or pronounced manner. A fire sacrifice, *yajna* was a primary ritual observed by Vedic Aryans. For that it was imperative to build a fire-altar, *vedi*. The *Shatapatha Brahmana* says:

> The altar has to be broader on the western side, narrow in the middle and broad again on the eastern side; for such a shape they praise a woman, who is broad at the hips, somewhat smaller between the

shoulders and narrowed in the middle (or around the waist), thereby making it (the altar) pleasing to the gods.

The *Chandogya Upanishad* also describes the entire sexual act as a ritual with its worldly rewards. It says:

Approaching (a woman with desire) is the syllable *him*; fascinating (courting, seducing) is the *prastava*; sleeping with the woman is the *udgita*; lying down with woman is *pratihara*; the passing of time (in love-making) is *nidhana*; and going to the end (fulfilment) is *nirvana* (death).

This is Vamadevya who is interwoven in the couple. One, who thus knows the Vamadevya as interwoven in the couple, becomes companioned, continues to copulate, attains the full span of lives, lives gloriously, becomes great in offsprings and cattle, great in fame. The *Brihadaranyaka Upanishad* says:

> One who approaches a woman with this knowledge acquires the fruit of *vajapeya yajna* and also *punya* (religious merit).

Mahavrata was a popular folk-festival that was adopted by Vedic priests who ritualised it. Woven into its fabric were ritual dancing, singing, music and a bit of play-acting too. It comprised of the ritual of an obscene dialogue exchanged between a celibate monk, *brahmachari*, and a woman of bad character, *pumschali*. Thus, runs the dialogue:

> The *harlot* says, "You, who have misbehaved, who have violated your vow of continence!"
>
> The *brahmachari* answers, "Shame on you, depraved one! Harlot who washes for the village community, who washes men's members!" (Sr. S. XI, 3.9)

This, the scriptures say, was followed by the act of copulation between Magadha and the harlot.

Ritualised obscenities of archaic fertility cults and religions have survived in later-day religious practices. Joseph Campbell, in his *Masks of Gods: Oriental Mythology* mentions an interesting ritual wherein the queen of *ashvamedha-yajna*-performing king sleeps with the sacrificial horse and indulges in obscene dialogues with the priests. He writes:

She lies down by the side of the dead horse, while the *adhvaryu* priest covers the two with cloth. He prays: 'In the heaven ye be covered, both and may the manfully potent stallion, seed bestower, bestow the seed within.'

The queen is expected to grasp and draw forth the sexual organ of the stallion, pressing it to her own.

"O mother, mother, mother!" she cries out. "Nobody will take me! The poor nag sleeps! Me, this wonderful little thing, all dressed in the leaves and bark of the Kampila tree!"

The priest says, "I shall incite the protector. Do thou too incite the protector."

Whereas the queen says to the stallion: "Come, let the two of us stretch out our limbs."

The priest prays to incite the God: "Come, lay thy seed well in the channel of the one who has opened to thee her thighs. O thou, potent of manhood, set in motion the organ that is to the woman the nourisher of life. It darts into the sheath, their hidden lover, darkly buffeting, back and forth."

The queen: "O mother, mother, mother, nobody is taking me."

The king adds an enigmatic metaphor, "Heave it high like someone leaning a load of reeds against the hill, winnowing in the fresh wind."

The priest turns to an attendant princess, pointing to her sex organ:

"The poor little hen there is splashing about in a flurry. The yard runs deep into the cleft; eagerly the sheath swallows."

And the princess says to the priest, pointing to his sex: "The poor little cock there is splashing about in a flurry, just like thy great big talkative mouth. Priest, hold thy tongue."

Once again repeats the queen: "O mother, mother, mother! No one is taking me!"

The supervising Brahmin calls down to her: "Thy father and thy mother once climbed to the top of the tree. 'Now,' called thy father, 'I am going to come across,' and he worked the yard in a deep cleft, going back and forth."

The queen wails: "O mother, mother, mother! No one is taking me!"

The hotri priest, turning to one of the other queens, says: "When that big thing in that narrow cleft bumps against the little thing, two large lips stir like two little fish in a puddle in a cow path."

> The addressed queen turns to the *adhvaryu* priest: "If the gods grant joy to that dripping, spotted bull, the woman's lifted knees will reveal it clearly as a truth before our eyes."
>
> And the queen repeats again: "O mother, mother, mother! No one is taking me!"
>
> The high priest now turns to the fourth wife, the Shudra: "When the noble antelope feeds on the barley seed, no one thinks of the village cow that fed upon it before. When Shudra's lover is an Aryan, she forgets the prostitute's fee."

The *Ramayana* informs us that when King Dasharatha of Ayodhya performed the horse sacrifice, the *ashvamedha yajna*, his chief queen spent a night with the sacrificial horse.

Bestiality scenes depicting the animal-woman relationship can be seen on medieval temples. Different animals including a dog, a boar, a donkey, are shown mounting women. These scenes might have been depictions of some fertility rituals.

In the *Atharva Veda*, certain magic spells are cited to beget the girl one desired. There is a hymn, described as the *kamabana sukta*, in which Kama, the god of love, is propelled to shoot arrows of love and hit the heart of the damsel to make her inclined favourably towards her lover. It says the desire for copulation and making love is denoted by the front portion of the arrow whose shaft is made up of a strong desire for nuptial enjoyment.

However, Kautilya in his *Arthashastra,* written in the fourth century BC, imposes some restrictions on the use of love spells, that fall under *kritya* or *abhichara,* black magic. He says:

> Witchcraft merely to arouse love in an indifferent wife or in a maiden by a lover or in a wife by her husband is no offence. But when it is injurious to others, the perpetrator is to be punished with a fine ranging between 200-500 *panas.* The one performing witchcraft to win over the sister of one's father or mother, the wife of a maternal uncle or of a preceptor, one's own daughter-in-law, daughter or sister has to have his limb cut off and also put to death. (*Indian Witchcraft* by Saletore)

In ancient vegetation and fertility cults, women played an

important role. It was believed that fertility in women affected the fertility of Nature. As a part of fertility rituals, it was common to perform intercourse with a woman in the field so as to ensure a bumper crop. On one of the Indus seals, about five-thousand years old, a tree is shown sprouting from the womb of a woman. The tree and the woman denote an eternal relationship in several rituals. It was believed that the Ashoka tree flowered only when kicked by a beautiful woman. These beliefs manifested in a ritual ceremony known as *Ashoka dohada*. In his play *Malvikagnimitra*, Kalidasa describes the ritual where the feet of a woman are painted with red lac and then anklets are worn over them, before she ceremoniously kicks the tree.

Different trees need different kinds of treatment by women. A verse in *Subhashitavali* says that the *kuvaraka* tree loves rubbing by the lovely breasts of a woman, *kucha-ghata-krida*. Trees like *maulisari* and *bakula* pined for a mouthful of wine or the ritual of *mukha-asava-sechanam*.

A woman and a tree motif were very popular in the early Indian art. Sculptures of *vrikshikas*, variously known as *shalabhanjika* or *yakshis* are found adorning the gateways of *stupas* at Bharhut and Sanchi.

The *shalabhanjika* or *yakshi* sculptures, even of folk deities like Chulakoka *devata* and Sirimao *devata*, are found to be half nude, completely nude or in diaphanous clothes. *Yakshas*, described as fertility deities or Nature's spirits, were offered meat, wine, incense, flowers, music, dance and drama.

Yakshis were considered to be the most beautiful creatures. Strange tales of their beauty and erotic behaviour are recorded in Buddhist *Jataka* tales. We come to know from some *Jataka* tales that beautiful *yakshis* would entice men passing through the forest, entertain them, make love to them and then kill them. *Yakshis* were described as cannibals. *Yakshi* Hariti was particularly fond of devouring children. It is believed that Buddha later reformed her.

Maybe initially the rituals of this archaic cult of fertility involved human sacrifices and sexual orgies. After performing sexual intercourse with the human prey, he might have been sacrificed in a gory ritual.

In the *Kadambari*, a prose-romance by Banabhatta, there is a description of a Kali temple situated deep in the forest. Its old priest was in possession of a book on *tantra*, written on palm leaves with red letters. It contained the *Mahakalamata* of old Pashupata variety. In it was described the formula for bringing under control a beautiful *yakshi* girl with the intention of making love to her. The old priest aspired to have the *yakshi* for himself.

Various rituals performed to unite with divine damsels are mentioned in Vedic literature. In the *Rig Veda*, we find the first recorded love story of the world. It is the story of a water-nymph Urvashi and King Pururava. The *Rig Veda* describes Urvashi as an *Apsara*. In later Puranic literature, *Apsaras* are described as charming seductresses in Indra's court.

In the *Shatapatha Brahmana*, a ritual is performed by which Pururava becomes a Gandharva and unites with Urvashi. The ritual has sexual overtones. Pururava constitutes the upper *arani*, churning stick for producing fire of *ashavattha* wood and the lower *arani* of *sami* wood which produces fire through friction between them. Offerings are made to that fire to become Gandharva and unite with Urvashi.

Archaic magico-religious rituals got permeated with mainstream religions like Hinduism, Jainism and Buddhism. Various *tantric* cults arose by absorbing these elements. The ritual of *pancha makaras* — *madya, mamsa, matsya, mudra* and *maithuna* — became common to many cults. Ancient fertility rituals as also tribal and folk ritual practices found their way in a number of small and big cults. Sex became a part of the rituals with a number of them becoming women-centric. The main aim of performing these rituals was to obtain occult powers, *siddhi*.

Pandit Somadevabhatta of Kashmir wrote a story book, *Kathasaritsagara*, in the tenth century. It was based on an earlier work written in Paishachi language and entitled *Brihatkatha*, by Gunadhya, belonging to the second century AD. Somadeva wrote about a terrible ritual performed by Queen Kuvalayavali in the royal seraglio.

The nude queen, sporting open hair and a big red vermillion mark on her forehead, sat in a magical circle drawn in different colours, muttering incantations with trembling lips. She made offerings of blood, liquor and human flesh.

She was initiated into this ritual by a Brahmin woman called Kalaratri. On the day of initiation, Kalaratri made Kuvalayavali, a young princess, take a purification bath and worship Ganesha. Stripping her clothes, Kalaratri made her sit in the magic circle and began offering incantations to Bhairava After bathing the princess again, she initiated her in the *dakini mantra* for obtaining *siddhi.* In the end, she made her eat human flesh. The ritual gave the princess the *siddhi* or the occult power of flying in the air. This power came to be known as *khechari vidya.*

In his play *Malati Madhava,* playwright Bhavabhuti speaks about attainment of *siddhi* in flying in air by practitioners of *kapalika* rituals. It is very interesting to note that Saudamini, a disciple of the Buddhist nun named Kamandaki, went on *kapalika sadhana* and climbed the mountain, *Sriparvata* to acquire miraculous occult powers. The playwright shows that she masters the *khechari vidya* and could fly through the air.

In the same play, we meet a terrible *kapalika* couple, Kapalakundala and her preceptor Aghoraghata, who reach the city of Padmavati from *Sriparvata* and choose to camp in the temple of Goddess Chamunda, who is also known as Karala, situated near a cremation ground. Kapalakundala by dint of her *sadhana* acquires the power to fly through air.

Yogini Tantra says that the cremation ground is the best place for performing rituals associated with the cult of Kapalika. Chamunda is an incarnation of Kali herself. *Manasara Shilpashastra* enjoins that the Kali temple should be built away from human habitation and close to a cremation ground where the *chandalas* live. The Chamunda temple near the cremation ground of Padmavati did not enjoy a good reputation; rather, the people feared the place. It was known as a place where living beings were sacrificed.

Sacrifice of young virgins to the deity was considered conducive to attaining *siddhi.* Kapalakundala kidnaps Malati, the beautiful and young heroine, and brings her to her preceptor, Aghoraghata, for sacrificing her to Goddess Chamunda Karala at the end of the ritual worship.

The *kapalikas* believed in *kamasadhana* and indulged in sexual-*yogic* rituals with their female partners. *Kapali* means Shiva; *kapalikas* are worshippers of Lord Shiva. The *kapalika* in the play says:

> Long live Shiva, the holder of *pinaka* (bow or trident), who wears a *vikrita* (a strange, abnormal) costume. It is he who taught us to achieve liberation through drinking wine and making love to a woman."

In the play *Prabodhachandrodaya,* written by Krishna Mishra Yati, an ascetic in the eleventh century, appears as a *kapalika* wearing a garland of human bones and heads. When asked about his religion, he replies that it comprises offering human flesh in the sacrifical fire, drinking wine from a human skull and sacrificing a human being by cutting his throat before offering to the Mahabhairava. "Can there be bliss and happiness without sensual enjoyment?" he asks. His consort, he states, was embodiment, *pratirupa* of Parvati herself. Jiva, who is Shiva's *swarupa,* embraces and sports with her.

The *kapalika* is accompanied by a voluptuous maiden called Kapaliki. When she embraces the Jain and Buddhist monks, they immediately convert themselves to the *kapalika* cult. The *kapalika* claims to have attained many *siddhis* this way.

A Buddhist monk in the play is shown flirting with the beautiful wives of his patrons. He says:

> Listen, O *upasakas* and *bhikshus,* all *sanskaras* are momentary; soul too is not permanent, hence if some *bhikshu* violates your women, you must not feel jealous. After all, jealousy is nothing but an impurity of the mind.

In the ninth century, Rajashekhara wrote a play entitled *Karpuramanjiri,* in which a *kapalika tantra*-guru named Bhairavananda appears. He is supposed to have possessed a number of occult powers. By his magical powers, he brings a beautiful princess by the name, Karpuramanjiri into the presence of

King Chandrapal. The princess had just emerged from her bath and was dripping with water. Explaining the tenets of his cult, he says:

> I do not know any *tantra* or *mantra*, nor do I have any preceptor to initiate me in the secrets of these *Shastras*. I drink wine, enjoy women by dint of which I achieve *moksha*. This is my *kuladharma*.
>
> Sluts, impetuous women glowing with passion, initiated in our cult are our consorts in religious rituals. We drink wine, eat meat, live on alms and sleep on a piece of leather.

He becomes so influential in the royal family that in the queen's pleasure garden, under a banyan tree, he builds a temple of Chamunda. He says that in *kala*'s (time) action of dissolution of all things, Chandi drinks the blood of living beings from the *kapala*, skull of Brahma.

This reference to *kapala* and the ritual of drinking blood out of it establishes the fact that Bhairavananda, devotee of Goddess Chamunda, was indeed a *kapalika*.

Some of the deities associated with sexual-religious practices were themselves very passionate and fond of wine, flesh and love-making. The dark, wild and fierce Goddess Kali is stated to be one of them. *Yogini Tantra* describes her as one wearing a garland of human skulls, nude, and with dishevelled hair. In her ears are ear-rings of two corpses and lips smeared with blood. Astride the corpse of Shiva, she stands above Mahakala. This supreme deity of left-handed Tantric sects, according to the *Kalika Purana*, is fond of having intercourse with Shiva in the inverted position (woman on top of the man), *viparitaratasakta*. Goddess Kali is propitiated by offering to her wine, flesh, fish and by performing certain sexual rituals.

There is a strong presence of the cult of mothers in India since the Indus Valley civilisation, and at times even beyond it. Goddesses are worshipped individually as also in groups. Durga is worshipped individually; a group of mothers known as *Sapta Matrikas* are worshipped together. The cult of Mother Goddesses gave rise to worship of numerous female deities and cults. One such cult was of deities known as *yoginis*. Sixty-four *yoginis* constitute a group.

Some of the *yoginis* have an animal-like countenance, but are sculpted into very beautiful and voluptuous females.

The *yoginis* as a group are generally referred to as the *yogini-chakra* or a circle of *yoginis.* In *Kathasaritsagara,* Bhairava is described as *chakreshvara* or head of the *yogini chakra,* which is also known as *matrichakra.* In a dense forest, the *yoginis* assemble together, worship *Bhairava* and then dance with him before vanishing into thin air.

In the same work, at another place, there is a reference to *yogini-chakra* that descends from the sky on to the cremation ground in search of corpses. When one is found, its heart is removed and offered to Bhairava.

The *yoginis* are perpetually drunk and move under the influence of liquor, as they are said to be fond of wine, human blood and flesh apart from all sexual pleasures.

Kalhana wrote *Rajatarangini,* the history of Kashmir, in the twelfth century. While describing the early history of Kashmir, he makes significant references to *yoginichakra* and its passionate longing for sexual enjoyment and drinking wine. He writes:

> And so, once, at midnight, Isana, who loses his sleep owing to anxiety over a miracle, smelt the perfume of divine incense. He heard an uncanny sound of the clang of many cymbals and bells strike violently along with the loud din of tambourines. On opening the window, he then saw *yoginis* standing inside a halo of light. Noticing their excitement and on finding that the skeleton has been removed, the startled Isana proceed to the funeral ground with his sword drawn. Thus he saw hidden behind a tree that the skeleton in the centre of the troupe of *yoginis.*
>
> With the rising tide of desire for sensual enjoyment with a lover, the nymphs drunk with liquor, having failed to find a virile man, had sought out the skeleton and carried it away.
>
> Each different limb was furnished from their own limbs and having from somewhere brought the male organ, in a moment, they thus set him up complete with all limbs.
>
> Next, the spirit of Sandhimat, which had been wandering about, not having taken possession of any other body, the *yogini's* having attracted by yoga placed it therein.

> Then, as he was being massaged with divine emollients, he woke as if from sleep and, at will, as a leader of the troupe, he had with them the joy in the way of love. (R.S. Pandit)

In the *Yogini Tantra*, there is a reference to a *yogini* who performed *raskrida* with Shiva in a mango grove. Even after vigorous sexual intercourse with Shiva, she remained insatiable.

Yogini temples are generally circular. Two temples at Ranipur-Jharial and Hirapur in Orissa, Mitauli near Gwalior in central India, Bhedaghat in Madhya Pradesh and Dudhai near Lalitpur are some of the circular *yogini* temples. The earliest *yogini* temples were built in Orissa around seventh or eighth century AD.

The *yoginis* were worshipped by observing esoteric rituals, including the five 'M's' to obtain the occult powers of *siddhis*. *Mahanirvana Tantra* says that worship without the five essential elements, *panchatatvas* — *madya* (liquor), *mamsa*(flesh), *matsya*(fish), *mudra* and *maithuna*(sexsual union) — is of no use. It is no wonder that rituals associated with the *yoginis*, who were highly passionate and fond of sexual pleasures, included practices such as drinking wine and conducting ritualistic orgies known as *chakrapuja*.

Vidya Dehejia in her book, *Yogini: Cult and Temples*, informs us that a series of rites and practices which constituted a part of *yogini* worship, are collectively known as *mahayaga*. Wine, flesh and blood as well as *shava-sadhana* or corpse ritual are included in *mahayaga*. But the most important ritual was *maithuna*, the sexual orgy, known as *yogini*- or *Bhairava-chakra*. The circular formation of *yogini* temples, she points out, helps in the formation of a circle of male-female couples who indulge in the *maithuna* ritual.

The *yoni* goddess, Kamakhya, on the Nilachal hill near Guwahati in Assam, is the heritage of archaic cult of worshipping the female procreative organ as part of a fertility ritual. The history of the *yoni* cult dates back to at least the Indus Valley civilisation where ring stones representing the female procreative organ were found during excavations.

On the Nilachal hill there is a cave, described as the *manobhava guha,* in the *Yogini Tantra.* In the cave, a *yoni* is sculpted on stone. A natural spring in the cave keeps the *yoni* symbol perpetually moist. Originally the tribals, such as the Kiratas and Shabaras, worshipped the *yoni* symbol which might not have been named as Kamakhya in the earlier times. There is evidence to show that the sacred space was later encircled by some kind of a wall, probably made up of bamboo or stone. Subsequently a temple was built on the cave. It was destroyed during the Muslim invasion of Assam in the sixteenth century. It was rebuilt in AD 1665, by King Naranarayana of Coch.

The *Puranas* as also works like the *Kalika Purana* and *Yogini Tantra* have woven several legends around the *Yoni* Goddess who in her new incarnation became Kamakhya.

It became a great *tantra-pitha* but as *Yogini Tantra* has said, the original Kirata *dharma* or rituals evolved by the Kirata tribals always prevailed. These included drinking of wine, eating of human flesh and fish, indulging in sexual orgies, wild dances. In the *Yogini Tantra,* Mahabhairava advises the devotees to go to the *yoni-pitha* on the hilltop to enjoy the company of the prostitutes worshipping Kali.

On the spiritual level, *maithuna* is defined as the union of *parashakti* with *atma* (soul). For *yogis,* says *Yogini Tantra, maithuna* is nothing but union of the *kundalini* with *saharadala padma.* But actually, *maithuna* too was not a taboo.

Maheswar Neog, in his book *Shankardeva and His Times,* gives us some very interesting information about the cult of Mother Goddesses of Kamarupa. He says:

> It is to be noted that in all temples of different forms of Devi on the Nilachala, the object of worship is no image, but in each a flat, slightly fissured stone, with water coming from below as in the case of the principal shrine of Kamakhya.

This leads us to the assumption that in the olden times, all over Kamarupa which was inhabited by Kiratas and other tribes, the *yoni* symbol was worshipped under different names by what we know today as Tantric rites, which included the offering of blood, animal sacrifices, wine, wild dances and sexual orgies. Gradually, the *Yoni* Goddess on Nilachala hill acquired prominence due to royal patronage and popular support. Even today, animal sacrifices are made on a large scale at the Kamakhya shrine. Vidya Dehejia, informs us that sexual orgies too are held regularly. She says:

> At Kamakhya, the *yoginichakra-puja* is performed on several auspicious days, such as the day of the vernal equinox, with *yogis* and *yoginis* sitting paired in a circle to perform this ritual. The followers of such rites are known as *adhikaris* (male) and *bhairavis* (females). *Meru tantra* tells us that it is a fundamental requisite for joy in this life and for rebirth as a God (*Yogini: Cult and Temples).*

Based on the material given in the *Kalika Purana* and *Yogini Tantra,* Dr Banikanta Kakati, in his book, *Mother Goddess Kamakhya,* discusses three ways of *yoni* worship. One is to mediate upon a sixteen-year-old beautiful, slightly drunk, nude goddess. Second is to worship Srichakra, a *yantra,* drawn on *bhurja patra* or a piece of silken cloth and third is a gold leaf etched with the female organ in the centre of another and consisting of a representation of nine such organs. In short, it means worship of a drawing of the female procreative organ. Uttar Kaulas, a branch of Shaktas, directly worship the organ of a beautiful living woman.

As noted by Aghonanda Bharati in his book, *Tantric Tradition,* in the final stages of the five 'M's' ritual, the *sadhaka* in a gesture of worship touches the *pudenta* of his Shakti, female partner, before the actual commencement of *maithuna* and recites the syllable 'M' one hundred times. This too can be taken as a form of *yoni* worship.

At Bhedaghat, probably Bhairavaghat of the yore, on River Narmada, there is a circular temple of sixty-four *yoginis.* The name of one of the *yoginis* in this temple is Kamada or giver of love. Vidya Dehejia writes:

> Below her lotus seat is an explicit scene of *yoni puja* or worship of female vulva, with the figures of attendants, devotees and musicians. Kamada is one of the names of Devi in *Kalika Purana* where Kama is identified with sexual love and it is specifically stated that Kamada takes away *jadya* or frigidity. *Yogini* Kamada is indeed the deity who gives sexual enjoyment.

Apart from animal sacrifice held daily at Kamakhya temple, there is yet another interesting ritual held here and it is *kumari puja* or virgin-worship. *Yogini Tantra* extols the ritual of virgin worship. A myth recorded by it says that Goddess Kali appeared before demon Kolasura in the form of a young girl and swallowed him along with his treasury, horses, elephants, chariots, army and his kith and kin. Since then, the custom of virgin worship, *kumari puja* commenced.

Kalika Purana says that virgins of all castes should be worshipped without any discrimination, though it is better if a worshipper by his good luck gets a virgin daughter from among the prostitutes for the ritual. Offerings of gold and silver should be made to her. If during the process of worship, the worshipper is struck with sexual desire, then he attains heaven. The worshipper achieves various forms of *siddhis* by worshipping virgins. Apart from intellectuals, *vidyadharis* and women of royal families, the beautiful women of gods, demons, *gandharvas, nagas* and *kinnaras* serve him and enjoy sexual pleasure as if it is with Bhairava himself.

The custom exists in different forms in different parts of the country. Devangana Desai, in her work *Erotic Sculpture of India,* writes:

> *Kumari puja* or worship of a young girl is an important tantric *ritual,* which is mentioned even by an orthodox tantra, like the *Mahanirvana tantra.* This ritual also reveals elements of fertility rites.

W. Ward, in 1822, described the practice of *kumari puja*, which, according to him; is too abominable to reach the ears of man.

> A maiden of any caste, below sixteeen years of age, is worshipped, sometimes, amidst an orgiastic ritual. She is offered liquor which is later partaken of as *prasada* by the worshippers. The priest, then, in presence of all, behaves towards this female in a manner which decency forbids me to mention; after which the persons present repeat many times the name of some God, performing actions utterly abominable...In *tantric* rites, called *dutiyoga,* any woman is worshipped as the Mother Goddess in the midst of secret ritualistic orgies.

Kumari puja is in a way extension of the custom of *yoni*-worship.

Another aspect of *yoni*-worship is the belief that Goddess Kamakhya menstruates in the month of *Saura Ashadha*. It is called *ambuvachi*. The cloth with red stains symbolises the menstrual blood of the *Yoni* Goddess and is given to the devotees. *Kubjika Tantra* calls this sacred cloth the Kamakhya *vastra*. A similar belief prevails in Orissa. It is believed that Mother Earth menstruates once a year for three days. All agricultural operations are stopped during this period.

The cult of *yoni*-worship has taken different forms. During excavations in Uttar Pradesh, Maharashtra, Karnataka and Andhra Pradesh, terracotta and stone pieces of nude headless females were found lying prostrate on their backs with legs outstretched, displaying their *yonis*. These were described as 'personified *yonis*' and some of them are preserved in state museums while some are found in temples. In the Badami taluka of Vijapur district of Karnataka, there is a place known as Nandikeshvar or Mahakut. In the Mahakut temple complex, this personified *yoni* can be found among the *Shivalingas*. It is known here as Goddess Lajjagauri. At Alampur in Andhra Pradesh, there is a famous Navalingeshvar temple. In the temple premises there is a small shrine with Lajjagauri as its presiding deity. This goddess is still worshipped in Siddhanakotte in north Karnataka as the goddess of fertility and barren women worship her so as to be able to beget children.

The earliest known personified *yoni* or Lajjagauri sculptures are dated to the first or second century AD. However, the cult is simply a variation of the ancient cult of Mother Goddesses which has a long history.

Phallic-worship too is as old as *yoni*-worship. The oldest known phallic stones belong to the Indus Valley civilisation. On one of the Indus seals excavated from Mohenjodaro, one can see a three-headed ithyphallic deity in a sitting posture, surrounded by animals.

A damaged limestone statuette from Harappa was considered by scholars to be ithyphallic. Benjamin Rowland in his book, *The Art and Architecture of India*, writes:

Another damaged statuette, also from Harappa, complements this

> torso in its striking forecast of iconographic and stylish elements of the historic periods of Indian art. This image, carved in greyish limestone, represents a dancing male figure, perhaps originally ithyphallic, with four arms and three heads. These attributes, together with the dancing pose, make it possible that this is a prototype of the later conception of Shiva as the lord of dance.

In the ancient world, the phallus was looked upon with awe and reverence, "as the mystical instrument of procreation, as a symbol of Nature, life-producing and inexhaustibly fruitful." It became synonymous with the mysterious procreative powers of Nature that brings forth life and keeps the human race going. Due to the pious awe it inspires, the phallus became a religious symbol to be worshipped with reverence.

In the Vedic period, there were tribes who worshipped Shisnadeva, the phallic deity. Shisnadeva and his followers are mentioned in the *Rig Veda* with disdain but it corroborates the existence of the phallic cult. In subsequent mythology, the phallus became the symbol of Shiva.

Shiva, in Hindu pantheon, is considered as many in one. He existed outside the pale of Vedic culture and grew with time, while assimilating the Vedic deity, Rudra in him. However, Shiva essentially remained a tribal deity worshipped by the tribals called Kiratas, Shabaras and the common people. In popular imagination he is a God, either nude or wearing a skirt of tiger skin, a serpent wrapped around his neck and his body smeared with ash, surrounded by ghosts, goblins and creatures which are half-human, half-animal. He gleefully dances in the cremation ground with a garland of human skulls around his neck. His other abode is the Kailasa peak in the Himalayas where he immerses himself in deep meditation or sports with his beautiful wife, Parvati. He is Mahadeva, the greatest among all divinities.

The aboriginal form of Shiva-worship survived in the Brahmaputra Valley. Ancient kings of Kamarupa, such as Banasura, were devotees of Shiva. He was propitiated with tribal rites. Maheshwar Neog, in his work, *Shankaradeva and his times* states:

> While starting on any military expedition against the Ahoms, the Koch king, Naranarayana (AD 1540-1584) performed such propitiatory rites to the deity (Shiva) as are prescribed in Hindu books. But Shiva, it is said, appeared before him in a dream and rebuked him severely for giving up his own tribal mode of worship. The king thereupon made arrangements for the performance of such rites by his Kachari soldiers on the banks of River Sonkos. Offerings (*upahara*) of ducks and pigeons, wine and cooked rice and sacrifices of buffaloes and swine, cocks and male goats were made. There were also Kachari dances with beating of drums (*madala*). It is added that the worship under the auspices of a Deodhani priest very effectively propitiates all gods.

As is evident from *Kalika Purana* and the *Yogini Tantra,* written in Kamarupa, Shiva's Bhairava form was more popular and was to be propitiated with *vamachari* rituals, that is, making him offerings of wine, flesh and ritual sex.

For the first time and that too unambiguously, the phallic connotation of Rudra Shiva is brought out in the *Mahabharata*'s 'Anushashana Parva'. It is here that we are told that Rudra Shiva is worshipped in the form of a *linga* or as *linga-yoni* combined. The epic says: *Pratyakshyamiha devendra pasya lingam bhagankitam.* Initially, it seems, the *linga-yoni* symbol was not what we see it as today — the *linga* held by the *yoni* — but was a *linga* marked by a *yoni.* On the phallic stone itself, the *yoni* symbol used to be carved.

The epic says no other god is worshipped in the form of a *linga* except for Shiva. The entire universe is manifested through the *linga* and *bhaga* or the male and female procreative organs respectively in which form Lord Shiva is worshipped. The entire human population is marked by either a *linga* or *bhaga.* This goes to show that it was known as Maheshvari *praja* or the population created by Shiva Maheshvara. All the women were created by Devi, hence possess the *bhaga* sign while males were created by Shiva and hence possess the *linga.* All women are manifestations of Devi while the men are of Ishana.

Shiva is described as one who sports a huge phallus, remains nude, hair on the body raised upwards and eyes strange and out of the ordinary. He is depicted sporting with daughters and wives of *rishis*.

According to a legend recorded in the *Brahmanda Purana*, once Shiva went to a hermitage, completely nude, and began to dance wildly. The wives of the *rishis* were so enchanted by him that they too started dancing with him in gay abandon.

According to *Nilamata Purana*, on the night of *Krishna Chaturdashi*, Kashmiri Shaivites offer special worship to Shiva. The whole night they sing and dance and make love to courtesans.

In the centre of the circular *yogini* temples, the shrines of Shiva or Shiva in his Bhairava form are located. The tantras of Kaula cult consider Shiva as the centre of *yoginichakra*. In the *Kathasaritsagara*, there is a reference to Bhairava dancing with *yoginis*.

The Devi temples in Kamarupa are invariably provided Bhairava shrines. The image of Shiva with Bhairava form was popular in Kamarupa.

In the *yogini* temple at Hirapur, there are four Bhairava images, all of which are ithyphallic. In the centre of the Ranipur-Jharial circular *yogini* temple in Orissa, there is a shrine of ithyphallic Shiva in the dancing pose. One of the early ithyphallic Shiva images was found at a village Asanpat, in Keonjhar district of Orissa and it is ascribed to the fourth century AD. Another interesting ithyphallic, dancing-Shiva image is seen adorning the eighth century Vetal temple at Bhubaneswar.

Lakulisha is considered the founder of the Pashupata sect. Ascribed to second century BC, he is considered to be an incarnation of Shiva himself. His images are shown in ithyphallic condition, *urdhvamudra* and are found all over the country.

Lakulisha was born in Lata country. Pashupatas are mentioned in the *Mahabharata*. The cult spread to many parts of the country. A number of inscriptions starting from the tenth century mention Lakulisha and his Pashupata cult. The cult received royal patronage.

In the seventh century, the Pallava king, Mahendra-vikramavarman of Kanchi wrote a farcical play named *Mattavilasprahasana*. In the play, there appears a character of

Pashupata named Babhrukalpa. He is angry with a Buddhist monk who tried to entice his beloved, a maid-servant of a barber, by showing her money concealed in his robe.

In Somadevabhatta's *Kathasaritsagara,* there is a Pashupata, who was given a sword kept in an invisible cave. One night, he performed the fire-ritual, a *havan,* and the cave became visible. The cave in fact was a palace made of precious stones, *asura-mandir.* After he got the magic sword, he acquired many occult powers, including the power to fly in air. He started living with a beautiful female *asura,* (a female demon) and took to excessive drinking.

The *vidhis* of Pashupatas were queer and some of them were actually obnoxious. Hiuen Tsang, in the seventh century, wrote that the Pashupatas smeared their bodies with ash and that they went naked and tied their hair in knots. Devangana Desai in her *Erotic Sculpture of India* finds the Pashupata influence on the early temples of Bhubaneswar replete with the erotic motif. She writes that an eleventh-century Rajrani temple, which is known for its erotic carvings, contains the images of Lakulisha seated in the company of Pashupata teachers.

Shaktas were devotees of the female principle in different forms. In left-handed or *vamachari* Shakta sects, sexual-religious rituals prevail. In a number of Shakta cults, Shiva stands as a companion of Shakti.

The ritualistic practices found in the *tantric* cult prevailed in this or that form in ancient India. Primitive belief in the efficacy of sexual-magical rites is at the core of many *tantric* cults. These ancient rites were supported by offerings of wine, flesh, dance, music, and even human sacrifices, to the divinities for acquiring *siddhis.* Alongside the *tantras* developed various theological and spiritual concepts, so much so that in some *tantras,* sexual rituals held only symbolic presence or were totally obliterated.

For the first time, the word *'tantra'* appears in the Gangadhara inscription of AD 423, and a verse from it runs as follows:

> Also for the sake of religious merit, the counsellor of the king caused to build this very terrible abode...and filled with female *ghouls* (*dakinis*) of the divine mothers (*matri*) who utter loud and full-

> throated shouts in joy, who stir up the ocean with the mighty wind rising from the magic rites of their religion (*tantra*).

Tantra basically was the religion of deities such as Mother Goddesses, *dakinis* (demonesses), *shakinis* and of terrible gods such as Bhairavas and *vetalas* whose worship included peformance of ritual orgies in cremation grounds. *Yogini Tantra* says that Shiva indulges in amorous sports with his female attendants in the cremation ground — *mahasmashane bhagavan kridate striganaih saha*. Different kinds of *chakras*, circular formations of amorous couples, were prescribed as modes of worship. All these rituals became permeated with *yogic* practices.

Tracing the evolution of tantric cults, Dr S.B. Dasgupta in his book, *Obscure Religious Cults* says:

> Side by side with commonly known theological speculations and religious practices, there has been growing in India an important religious undercurrent of esoteric *yogic* practices from a pretty old time; these esoteric practices, when associated with the theological speculations of the Shaivas and Shaktas, have given rise to Shaiva and Shakta *tantricism*, which, when associated with Buddhistic speculations, have given rise to the composite religious system of Buddhist *tantricism;* and again, when associated with the speculations of Bengal Vaishnavism, same esoteric practices have been responsible for the growth of the esoteric Vaishnavite cult known as the Vaishnava Sahajiya movement. Similarly we have Saura and Ganapatya *tantras* associated with the worship of Surya and Ganapati.

Ganapati belongs to the Shaiva pantheon and is worshipped with reverence throughout the country. In the *Gatha Saptashati*, ascribed to the first or second century AD, there is a reference to a woman indulging in amorous sports with men, taking the image of Ganapati under her head as a pillow. This may be some kind of sexo-religious ritual, according to some scholars.

N.P. Joshi in his *Bharatiya Murtishastra* refers to the early images of Ganesha — one from Sankisa in Uttar Pradesh and three in the Mathura Museum — all of which are in the nude. He then refers to the Ganesha image from Udayagiri in Madhya Pradesh and another at Shor Bazar in Kabul, both ithyphallic and belonging to the Gupta period. It seems that images of Shakti Ganesha and Ucchistha Ganesha were worshipped by the *tantrics*.

In the *Padma Purana*, devouts are enjoined upon to donate young, beautiful girls adorned with fine jewellery to ascetics, probably for performing tantric rituals. On a number of medieval temples, such as the Vishvanatha temple and the Duladeva temple at Khajuraho, and the temples at Modhera, Roda, Halebid and Bagali, we find sculptural depictions of ascetics performing ritual sex with their female partners.

Devangana Desai feels that remnants of ancient fertility rites are found in tantric rituals. She writes in her book, *Erotic Sculpture of India*:

> *Chakrapuja* or worship in a circle seems to be an example of the survival of fertility rites in *tantricism*. It is an orgiastic festival conducted under the leadership of a guru. The *Hevaraj Tantra* of about eighth century says that feasting in a circle fulfils the substance of all desires. One should set about this feasting in a cremation ground or in a mountain cave in a deserted town or in some lonely place. As described in the *tantric* work, *Kaulavalinirnaya*, an equal number of men and women, without distinction of caste and blood relationships, secretly meet at night and sit in a circle. The goddess is represented by a *yantra* or a mystical diagram. Women cast their bodices in a receptacle which is taken by men in turns. The woman whose bodice is received by the man becomes his partner in the sexual ritual. The sexual ritual is preceded by a long sequence of *pujas* and *vratas* to propitiate the deity.(p.118)

In the book, *Erotic Sculpture of India*, this procedure of picking up bodices from the receptacle is popularly known as *ghata-kanchuki-vidhi*.

During the course of its evolution, the old schools of *tantra* established a very elaborate and complicated system of rituals and pedantry. This was resented and new ways, free from *japa*(meditation), *tapa*(austerity), *mantra*, *mandalas* and *yantras*(which are objects that help concentration during meditation), were explored by some *sadhakas*. The *Srisamaj Tantra* says:

> It is futile to torture oneself by forsaking the pleasures of the five sense organs. If you torture your body with severe austerities, it will disturb your mind and you cannot attain *siddhi* when you are in a disturbed state of mind.

In Rajashekhara's play, *Karpuramanjiri*, Bhairavananda, the *tantra* guru bluntly says:

> I know not any *mantra* or *tantra*, nor any spiritual knowledge.
> I did not learn the technique of meditation by the grace of guru.
> We drink wine and enjoy the company of women and thus achieve liberation.

Out of this attitude many sub-sects emerged on the scene and these mostly contributed to moral degradation of the *sadhakas*.

Buddhist *tantras* date back to great antiquity. According to some scholars, the Buddha himself introduced the tantric elements in his teachings. After the Buddha, the secret conclaves of monks practicing *tantric sadhana, guhyasamaja* appeared on the scene. They indulged in all sorts of sexo-*yogic* practices. *Guhyasamaja Tantra* was written and it permits the use of *pancha* 'M'-*karas* and performance of a number of esoteric rituals including *mantras, mudras, mandalas*, etc.

This form of Buddhist *tantrism* evolved into a school of *tantra* known as *Vajrayana*. Side by side, *Sahajayana* appeared on the scene. Their *sadhana* included selection of a beautiful woman of low caste. She was called a *mahamudra* or *prajna* and the followers indulged in ritual sex with her.

Commenting on the Sahajayana school, Dr N.K. Sahu, in his work *Buddhism in Orissa*, writes:

> The *Sahajayana* remains a way of propitiating the primitive instincts and desires, i.e. the sex hunger and like, and in advocating the principle, it challenges all established religions with their rigour of discipline, orthodoxy and formalities.

The *Advayasiddhi* asserts:

> There is no need of undertaking pain by fasting and observing rites,

> nor is there any need for bathing and purifying the body, as well as observing any traditions and formalities whatsoever.

Luipa declares:

> Of what consequences are all the processes of meditation? In spite of all these, one has to die in weal and woe. Discard all the elaborate practices of *yogic bandha* and false hopes for supernatural gifts and take up the cause of *sunyata* as your own.

Thus, *Sahajayana* appears as an open protest to all sorts of religious formalism and *yogic* rigours, and it lays emphasis on developing human nature for realisation of the ultimate truth, *sunyata*.

The *Sahajayanas* even denounce the practice of worship of gods and goddesses as advocated by *Mahayana* and *Vajrayana*, while at the same time they assert that all such gods and goddesses, including Lord Buddha, reside in the body of man.

Says Saraha:

> The scholars explain all the scriptures, but fail to know that Buddha resides in the body. So the *Sahajayanas* profess the principle of satisfying all the needs of the physical body, which is the abode of all the *tattvas*, *piyhas*, the deities, and without which no *siddhi* can be obtained.This idea of worshipping the physical body is quite in keeping with the principle of propitiating human nature with its sex passions and other primitive propensities...the whole *yogic* process of *Sahajayana* school is found to be based on a highly sublime aspect of the sex, where the *sadhaka* is to embrace and sport with the female Shakti, variously called as the Chandali, Dombi, Savari, Yogini, Niratma Sahaja Sundari, etc. The bliss that comes out of these sexo-*yogic* practices is generally divided into four stages and the final stage is called *mahasukha*.

In *Shaktas*, it was Shiva and Shakti; in Buddhist tantric cults, it was *Prajna* and *Upaya* and in Vaishnavas, it was Radha and Krishna.

The *Vaishnava Sahajiya* cult arose in Bengal before the emergence of Chaitanya. According to P.C. Bagchi, the earliest reference to *Sahajiyas* is found in the inscription of the thirteenth century and is known as the Mainamati plate. Chandidasa was the earliest known and prominent *Vaishnava Sahajiya*. He was a great love-poet of the fourteenth-century Bengal. He performed the *Sahajiya sadhana* of love with a washer-woman, *rajaki* named Rami.

> In Sahaja Vaishnavism, love was conceived as *sahaja*. This *sahaja* or the absolute playfully divides itself into two — the lover and the beloved, the enjoyer and the enjoyed, as Krishna and Radha. This playful division of the one into two is for nothing but for self-realisation. In terms of Sahajiyas, the *sahaja* manifests itself into two currents: *rasa* (love) and *rati* (the exciting cause of love and the support of love) which are currents represented by Krishna and Radha. Again, it is held that man and woman on earth are but physical representations of Krishna and Radha, or *rasa* and *rati* of Gokola; in the corporeal forms man and woman represent *rupa* or the external manifestation of Krishna and Radha, who reside, so to speak, in every man and woman as *swarupa* or the true spiritual self. The *sadhana* comprises first of realisation of *swarupa* in *rupa* and after this realisation, the pair should unite in love. The realisation of infinite bliss that follows from such a union is the highest spiritual gain. (S.B. Dasgupta).

The *Sahajiyas* extolled the ideals of *parakiya* love or love between a man and woman who is not his own, because in such a relationship, the degree of passion is very high. The Sahajiyas claim that poet Jayadeva, Chaitanya and his ardent followers like Rupa and Sanatana practiced *Sahajiya sadhana*. They say Sathi, daughter of Sarvabhauma, was Chaitanya's companion in this *sadhana*, but some scholars take this claim as nothing but as an effort of the Sahajiyas to acquire respectability.

A very strong streak of asceticism prevailed in all major Indian religions, such as Hinduism, Buddhism, and Jainism. Probably these love rituals were a form of revolt against the strict regimentation imposed by these ascetic religious practices.

Chapter Five

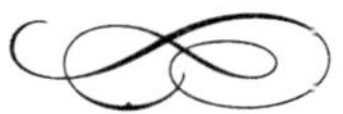

Art of Love

Love became the theme of art since early times. The history of Indian erotic art dates back to hoary antiquity and early glimpses of which can be seen in the pre-historic cave paintings, the earliest among them dated to twenty thousand BC.

In one of the early cave painting sites at Bhimbetka, we find a beautiful sketch of a copulating couple in unusual postures. In the Kathotia cave painting, dated to the Chalcolithic period, we see a large group of phallic dancers with huge, erect penises. One of them is seen lying on the ground, indulging in auto-eroticism. This points to the tradition of performing nude phallic dances and subsequently painting them.

When we come to the Indus Valley civilisation, apart from ring stones and phallic stones, we find several terracotta images of nude women identified as Mother Goddesses. Probably the tradition of making secular female sculptures had its origin in the sculptural representations of female deities.

But the most fascinating metal-work of the Indus period is a statuette of a slender girl in a provocative posture. This entirely nude female sculpture is a secular piece of ancient art found at Mohenjodaro. The sculpture is that of a dancing girl. Another piece, a torso of a statuette carved in limestone, found at Harappa, is identified as that of a nude, probably an ithyphallic, dancer.

The two Indus statuettes of dancers point to a tradition of nude dance performances.

As we have already seen, the tradition of erotic paintings dates back to the days of cave art. In the Buddhist *Maha Ummagga Jataka*, there is a reference to erotic paintings done on the walls of a palace to depict six heavenly spheres for sexual pleasures.

In yet another *Jataka* tale, we are told that in the picture gallery of King Videha, love-postures of different kinds were executed skilfully by the court artists. Scholars ascribe the *Jataka* tales to sixth century BC.

Bharata in his *Natya Shastra,* ascribed to second century BC, speaks of decorating the theatre hall with men and women in erotic postures, *latabandha*. Vatsyayana says that when a woman embraces a man, just as a creeper embraces a *shala* tree, it is called *latavestitaka*. In his *Kamasutra* written in the third century AD, Vatsyayana speaks of erotic paintings of couples, *mithuna chitra*. In the chapter titled '*Dutikarmanrakarna*', Vatsyayana says that the girl to be seduced should be shown erotic paintings depicting intercourse — *chitransuratasambhogananyasamani darshayet*.

Giving information about the tradition of erotic paintings in her book *Erotic Sculpture of India*, Devangana Desai writes:

> Bana, describing the love-chamber of the newly wed royal couple, mentions that erotic paintings presumably were meant to be seen by the shy bride. On the doors of this chamber were portrayed the goddesses, Rati and Priti, the consorts of Kamadeva. One of the paintings on the wall depicted the god of love aiming his shaft near a red Ashoka tree (*Harshacharita*).... Kings and wealthy people also commissioned artists for preparing illustrated series on erotics and love lyrics... In the eleventh century, King Bhoja of Malva, in his *Samaranganasutradhara,* mentions specifically that monuments should be adorned with women engaged in amorous sports, *ratikrida*, and *nayaka* or hero desirous of sex play.

This tradition was inherited by various schools of miniature paintings.

Can there be any more luscious, soft and inspiring canvas in the world than the tender breasts of a lovely girl for the artist to work on? Of course not, says the ancient Indian lover who is adept in the art of body decoration. His creative imagination is at its peak when he uses his brush dipped in rainbow colours on the lovely body of his beloved.

We do not know exactly when the romance of body painting started. It must have been of tribal origin. In pre-historic cave paintings, we see men and women with their bodies decorated with colours. Vatsyayana, in his *Kamasutra*, mentions the art of body painting, *angaranga*. Though he describes in detail how to decorate the body of a woman by drawing different diagrams and figures with the help of nails during love-making, he is silent about the use of colours and paints except for saying that "*dashana-vasana-angaranga*" is one of the sixty-four arts.

In Sanskrit and Prakrit poetry, several references are made to body decoration. In the *Kumarsambhava*, poet Kalidasa writes that while preparing beautiful Parvati for her marriage ceremony, her female friends decorate her lovely body with *gorochana*.

However, breast painting was an art practiced by privileged lovers only.

In the *Gatha Saptashati*, there are references to breast paintings. A verse says:

> Feel not too proud, friend, for your lover painting a love letter on your breasts; had the hands of my lover not shook when overwhelmed by excessive passion, he too would have decorated my bosom with love paintings!

In the last section of *Gita Govinda* of Jayadeva, there is a lovely song, *'kuru yadunandana...'*, in which beautiful Radha commands Krishna to do her biddings after making love to him. In it, she commands her lover, Krishna, to paint her breasts. She says:

> Paint, O Krishna, with fingers cooler than sandalwood, leaves and flowers, with musk, on this breast, which resembles a vase of consecrated water, crowned with fresh leaves and placed near a vernal bower to propitiate the god of love!

This verse gives us an idea of the types of paintings done on breasts. Leaves and flowers were favoured subjects and they were painted with musk. The theme of painting breasts by the lover is commonly seen in miniature paintings.

Another type of love painting mentioned by Vatsyayana is one in which leaves are drawn with the nail. This art is known as *patracchedyakriya.* He says that couples engaged in amorous sports, *maithunas,* should be drawn on leaves of the trees. In Kalidasa's celebrated play, *Abhijnana Shakuntala,* the heroine Shakuntala is seen writing a love-poem on the leaf of a lotus plant addressed to her lover, Dushyanta.

India is famous all over the world for its erotic sculptures adorning the numerous temples of medieval period, as seen at Konark and Khajuraho. However, the history of erotic art dates back to several centuries earlier. In her book *Erotic Sculpture of India,* Devangana Desai writes:

> The depiction of coital couples and orgies is seen in terracottas of Chandraketugarh and Tamluk dating from circa second century BC onwards and in those at Kaushambi and Bhita of the second to first century BC... At Chandraketugarh, the various poses of sexual congress include frontal congress, oral congress of fellatio type, congress from rear, head-down pose, sitting pose, standing pose and sleeping congress on the bed. There are scenes showing erotic group activity... The earliest depictions of *mithunas* in stone art is seen in second century BC monuments at Sanchi and Bharhut.

The tradition of sculpting sensuous women began during the era of Indus Valley civilisation — the copper statuette of a nude dancer in a provocative pose discovered at Mohenjodaro being one of the early examples.

Incidentally, India's earliest dated art work of human origin was a small, delicate, female figurine of bone found in the Belan Valley of Mirzapur district of Uttar Pradesh and which is dateable to 20,000 BC.

It was during the Mauryan period that gradually stone became the medium of sculptural art. A full-sized statue of a voluptuous *yakshi* of Maurya period was found at Didargunj, Patna. With her full breasts, broad hips and thin waist, she formalised the concept of female beauty which was more or less followed by later sculptors.

The *yakshi*, famous as *Yakshi* Chamaradharini, is seen wearing ear-rings, a number of bangles on both her hands and anklets on her feet. A beaded girdle encircled her round hips. The pendant of her necklace dangles in the deep crevice of her heavy breasts. The stone surface is polished to such a perfection that apart from the softness and warmth of the female flesh and the texture of her skin, it displays youthful exuberance of a woman in her prime.

Yakshis are known as Nature's spirits, fond of drinking wine and love-making. They are considered to be very beautiful. Describing a *yakshi* in his romantic poem, *Meghadoota* (The Cloud Messenger), Kalidasa writes:

> She was slim, of swarthy complexion, having sparkling teeth like jasmine buds, lips red like *bimba* fruits, attenuated at the waist, with eyes like a frightened deer, a deep navel, slow of gait due to the weight of her heavy hips, slightly bent forward due to the pull of her full breasts.

Kalidasa further adds that she was the first and the best in the creation of feminine beauty by the Creator.

Yakshis in translucent clothes adorning the gateways of the great Buddhist *stupa* at Sanchi and ascribed to the Sunga period are seen frankly displaying their feminine charms, leaving nothing to the imagination. Particularly beautiful is a *yakshi* figure at the eastern gate entwined around the mango tree. In the same tradition are the nude, semi-nude *yakshis* in different postures embellishing the uprights of the railings, once forming a part of the *stupa*, and now housed in the Mathura Museum. The railing pillars with lovely *yakshis* were excavated at the Bhutesar mound at Mathura and are ascribed to second century AD. These *yakshi* sculptures are known for their "flamboyance and sensuality of expression." On the upper portion of the railings, amorous couples are carved.

The tradition of decorating Buddhist monuments, like the ones at Sanchi, Bharhut, Amaravati with images of beautiful women in different postures, fully clad, semi-nude or nude, spread to temples and shrines of other religions like Hinduism and Jainism. Even *shalabhanjika* or the woman-and-tree motif on early Buddhist monuments is seen on the monuments of Hindus and Jains.

It is always very interesting to trace the origin of the art motif. On a seal belonging to the Indus Valley civilisation era, we can see a tree sprouting from the womb of a woman. The close connection between a woman and tree is seen on a number of seals in different forms. Probably the *shalabhanjika* or early Buddhist monuments might have their origin in the seals of the Indus era showing a similar concept. However, the motif was explained in Buddhist terms with the help of a legend. It is said that Queen Maya gave birth to the Buddha in a standing position, holding on to a branch of *shala* tree with one hand for support.

To this was added another concept known as *dohada*. It was believed that trees like Ashoka pine for the touch of a beautiful woman or for wine sprinkled on it by her with her mouth. Flowering of such trees takes place only when the ritual of *dohada* is performed by women. This again points at the importance of a woman in the fertility rituals of the yore.

In ancient times, the woman was at the centre of all agricultural operations. All this took the form of the *shalabhanjika* motif. Broadly speaking, religious monuments had two types of icons — sacred and secular. The form of sacred icons was decided according to the strict tenets of iconography devised by any particular religion to which it belonged. However, secular icons were mainly for decorative purposes and artists were free to use their creative imagination or simply follow the trend set by the earlier masters.

The beautiful sculptures of shapely and alluring women, variously known as *shalabhanjika*, *yakshi*, *apsara*, *surasundari*, *devangana* started appearing in profusion on monuments as embellishing icons.

Erotic icons travelled over time from *mithuna* to *maithuna*. *Mithuna* means couples. Simple couples, at the most holding hands, gradually started becoming bold and sensuous before resorting to kissing, embracing and similar intimate acts. Then they graduated to sexual intercourse in different postures, *maithuna*. The early simple *mithunas* of second to first century BC are mostly seen on Buddhist monuments, such as those at Bharhut and Karle, before becoming intimate gradually. At the beginning of sixth century, the sculptures are shown indulging in sexual acts. The tendency reached its peak around the tenth to the thirteenth century, as seen in the temples at Bhubaneswar, Puri, Konark and Khajuraho.

And what a variety of intimate postures, attitudes, compositions — you name them, imagine them, they are there for you to see. You see simple or complex one-man-one-woman coitus, a couple performing gymnastic feats while enjoying sex, orgies, oral sex, auto-erotic, music and dance as adjuncts to the sexual act. Even ascetics are shown enjoying sex with female partners in various postures.

Here you may ask, why was there so much, so varied depiction of sex on religious monuments and temples, in the medieval period?

Some scholars attribute this to the influence of tantric cults. Though originating in the distant past, tantric cults started making their presence felt from the fifth century AD. A number of them included *maithuna* along with drinking of wine, eating of fish and flesh as the major ingredients of their *sadhana*. They claimed that *maithuna* led the *sadhaka* to liberation.

Grihyasamaja Tantra propounds a theory that *sadhana* which is difficult, painful and bound by severe rules and regulations can lead the *sadhaka* nowhere. One can attain *siddhi* by enjoying all kinds of sensuous pleasures. True knowledge is acquired by such enjoyment, the chief among them being intercourse with a woman, leading to supreme bliss — *strisukham param*.

Shaktas declare *maithuna* as the *parama tatva* or the ultimate principle. Through *maithuna,* one can attain supreme knowledge — *brahmajnana*. Enjoyment of sensual pleasure is yoga itself — *bhoga yogayate sakshat. Mahanirvana Tantra* says that worship without the *panchatatvas* — *madya, mamsa, matsya, mudra* and *maithuna* — is of no use.

Though the *tantras* stressed the importance of copulation, they did not contain the prescription of sexual postures. The *mudra* of *panchatatva* means the ritualistic gestures but certainly not sexual postures. Then from where did the sexual postures as depicted on medieval temples, arise? And why did *mithuna* and *maithuna* sculptures become a part of temple buildings?

Some scholars think that they were a part of the scheme of embellishing religious buildings. Their main purpose was decorative, not ritualistic. Expression of pure aesthetic delight — *rasa*, a condition of becoming — *bhava*, particularly an erotic emotion of love and longing — *sringara*, was their main aim. These sculptures belong to the secular and not the religious or tantric tradition and the sculptors drew their inspiration from Sanskrit literature which described feminine graces and works like *Natya Shastra* and *Kamasutra*, which speak of artistic as well as erotic postures.

In this case, we will be required to presume that the sculptors, stone-cutters, *shilpis* were well conversant with the *Natya Shastra*, *Kamasutra* and Sanskrit dramatic as well as poetic works, though it seems to be a distant possibility.

This class of people, in ancient times, had close contact with *ganikas*, who were well versed in arts and literature. Through *ganikas*, this knowledge might have percolated down to the *shilpis*, who might have invented or devised their own forms that became a part of their trade.

Devadasis might have acted as natural models for sculptors working at temple sites. It was in the fourth century BC that Kautilya mentioned the *devadasis* in his *Arthashastra*. The very first inscription mentioning a *devadasi* at Jogimara cave on Ramgiri hill in Madhya Pradesh and belonging to the second century BC, very clearly mentions her love affair with none else but the sculptor. The inscription says:

> Sutanuka by name, a *devadasi*.
> Sutanuka by name, a *devadasi*.
> Excellent among young men love her,
> Devadinna by name, skilled in sculpture.

The ornaments, costumes, dance postures, graceful attitudes were possibly copied by the sculptors, like Devadinna. A tenth-century Bayana inscription of Chitralekha speaks about the dancing skills and the beauty of the *devadasis* "whose eyes were like petals of lotus flowers, whose hips were heavy and whose faces were like the moon." So enchanting were the girls of the temple, says the inscription, that "owing to the temptation of seeing them, the enemy of Madhu (Vishnu) does not leave his own image for a moment nor does he now remember the heavenly damsels like Rambha and others."

They were skilled dancers. *Nata mandirs*, dancing halls, were added for their performances. One hundred and eight dance postures given by Bharata in his *Natya Shastra* are known as *karanas* and were sculpted on temples like Brihadishwara at Tanjore for the guidance of the temple dancers. According to an inscription in the temple, about four hundred *devadasis* served Brihadishwara of Rajaraja Chola.

Chapter Six

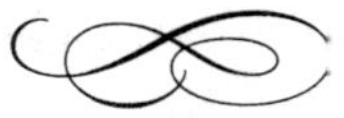

POETRY OF LOVE

Early Indian poetry, collectively known as Vedic poetry, is considered as sacred writing, scriptural in nature. However, we find that there are references in it made to sexual behaviour and norms of the Vedic people. Instances of sexual immorality, including adultery and incest, are mentioned, sometimes in story form. Elopement of wives and paramours is mentioned along with that of unwed mothers and prostitutes. The moral code for sexual behaviour was formulated by the Vedic seers. In a nutshell, immoral practices included:

> Criminal conversation of a man with the female friend of a female guru, with a female friend of male guru, with any married woman, conversation with such a degraded person, incestuous sexual union with female relatives of one's mother or father, with sister or their female issues, causing abortion, looking at the naked wife of another man, a man's wife having a paramour, a married woman running away from her husband, one man touching or molesting another man's wife, giving birth to illegitimate children (*Society in Ancient India*, p. 181).

In the *Chandogya Upanishad,* there is the touching story of a young boy, Satyakama, whose mother, Jabala, had served many men in her young age. Jabala's son Satyakama once approached her and told her that he wanted to learn the Vedic lore at the feet of a guru. He then asks Jabala if the guru were to ask who his father was and what was his *gotra* (sub-sect), what should he tell him? Jabala replied that she herself did not know this, but added, "If asked, tell the guru that you are Satyakama Jabala."

Satyakama went to Haridrumat Gautam and humbly appealed to him to teach the *Vedas*. Haridrumat Gautam said that he could not teach anybody without knowing his *gotra*. Satyakama truthfully told him that neither he nor his mother knew about the *gotra* of his father because they did not even know who his father was. He was just a son of Jabala — Satyakama Jabala.

Highly impressed by his truthfulness, Haridrumat Gautam accepted Satyakama Jabala as his disciple. Later, he became very famous as a great guru and Vedic scholar.

India's history of literature starts with epics like the *Ramayana* and the *Mahabharata*. Tradition describes *Ramayana* as an *adi kavya* or the first work of poetry. It was composed by Maharshi Valmiki and is essentially a biography of Prince Rama of Ayodhya. It is believed to be composed sometime before the advent of the Buddha, eighth to sixth century BC. We do not find much of erotic content in this epic. In the *'Ayodhyakanda'*, a chapter, there is a description of Bharata, brother of Rama, and his soldiers being regaled by Bharadwaja Muni in his *Prayagvana* with wines and liquors like *maireyaka* and *sura*. Then they are entertained for one whole night by the *apsaras*, with their singing, dancing and amorous sports. The entire chapter presents a bacchanal scene.

In the *'Sundarkanda'*, another chapter, there is an erotic description of beautiful women sleeping under the influence of liquor in the harem of Ravana. There is a passing reference to amorous sports and love-making between Rama and Sita on their return to Ayodhya after killing Ravana. It is said that to enjoy themselves, they went to the pleasure-garden in the palace, Ashoka *vatika*, and sat on seats decorated with flowers. Rama with his own hands gave intoxicating drinks, *madhu* and *maireyaka* to Sita to drink. Beautiful girls under the influence of wine danced around the royal couple to entertain them. Thus, the entire night of *Shishira ritu* was spent in amorous sports.

The *Ramayana* speaks of the *rakshasa* culture of abducting and kidnapping beautiful girls and raping them. Once Ravana, while moving aimlessly in the forests of Himalayas, sees a very beautiful and young girl, Vedavati, performing penance. Overcome with passion, Ravana tries to rape her but she jumps into the fire.

In another incident, Ravana reaches the Kailasa mountain. His passion gets aroused on observing the unique scenic beauty of the region. Suddenly he sees Rambha, one of the best among the *apsaras*, adorned in a dazzling costume and jewellery. She is extremely beautiful. Her face is like a full moon, eyebrows like a curved bow and her legs resemble the trunk of an elephant. Her hips and loins are covered with beads of *mekhala* tied around her waist. She wears a blue saree and is bedecked with fragrant flowers of all the six seasons. Struck by Cupid's arrow, Ravana grasps her hand and asks,

> "Who is the one that will taste the nectar of your lovely lips? Who is going to touch your full breasts that look like two pitchers of gold? Who is going to mount on your *jaghana* which is like heaven itself? Whose desire you are going to fulfill today? Who is that fortunate one? But certainly he cannot be as powerful as Ravana. Hence surrender to me."

Rambha tells him that she is on her way to meet her lover Nalakubar, son of Kubera, the king of *yakshas*. But Ravana does not listen to her pleas and forcibly rapes her.

There is a passing reference to the custom prevalent among the members of the actor community of lending their wives for sexual pleasures. There is a story of Ahalya, the beautiful wife of Sage Gautama, whom Indra, the king of gods, tries to seduce by appearing before her in a guise. Ahalya allows him to make love to her for mutual pleasure.

Though not much of the erotic element is found in the *Ramayana*, it is present in abundance in the eleventh-century Rama story based on a play *Hanumanataka*. In its second act, the playwright describes the amorous sports of Sita and Rama in a very sensual style. At some places, the description even tends to become obscene.

The epic, *Mahabharata* was composed by Maharishi Vyasa as an *itihasa* or a historical fiction to tell the story of a major conflict between cousins, the Kauravas and Pandavas, and the fierce war for succession to the throne. Lots of extraneous material has been added to the original work of Vyasa, so much so that the original Bharata became the *Mahabharata*. Composed before the sixth century BC, it acquired its present form around the fourth century AD. It is a veritable encyclopaedia of Indian culture. Writing about it, Maurice Winternitz states:

> In reality, one can speak of the *Mahabharata* as an epic and a poem in a very restricted sense. Indeed, in a certain sense, the *Mahabharata* is not at all a poetic product, but rather, an entire literature.

Draupadi, daughter of Drupada, king of Panchala, is the heroine of the epic, and extremely beautiful. Having a lustrous complexion like blue sapphires, her eyes like lotus petals, her hair long and curly, her shapely body emits the fragıance of blue lotus. She is married to Prince Arjuna in a *swayamvara,* a marriage ceremony wherein the girl can choose the man she wants to marry amongst those assembled by garlanding him. Howerver, when the other Pandava brothers see her, they too get struck by Cupid's arrows and perforce Draupadi becomes the wife of the five Pandava brothers, dividing her time among them. This is rather unusual, though the *Mahabharata* explains this with the help of a myth. According to the *Kamasutra*, it was the Panchala school of Babhravya which professes that a virgin loses her chastity only if she has sex with more than five men.

The sexual mores of the day were decided by the circumstances. For instance, when the Kuru king of Hastinapura, Vichitravirya, dies without producing an heir, his young and beautiful wives, Ambika and Ambalika, are forced to cohabit with Vyasa, their brother-in-law. Vyas is very ugly. When he arrives in the bedroom of Ambika, she closes her eyes with fright and aversion; and when he visits Ambalika, she is so frightened that her complexion turns pale. It is no less than rape, with consent though. They do produce children but one is blind and the other is born very pale and is named Pandu.

Pandu marries Princess Kunti and becomes the king of Hastinapura. After some time, he goes to the forest, leaving the throne to his blind brother Dhritarashtra. Due to a curse, he is unable to cohabit with either of his wives — Kunti and a very beautiful Madri. With the consent of her husband, Kunti invites the gods to cohabit with her. The younger queen, Madri, follows suit and they together have five sons known as the Pandavas.

Unmarried Kunti, while living in her father's house, gives birth to a son by the grace of the sun-god, Surya.

Love stories are present in the epic, but seldom is there any erotic description as such. It is said in the *Udyog Parva* that just before the commencement of the Bharata war, an inebriated Krishna and Arjuna sat in the tent of Arjuna, whose legs lay on the thighs of Satyabhama, wife of Krishna, and Krishna's legs on the thighs of Draupadi, wife of Arjuna. Children were forbidden to enter inside.

In the 'Khandavadaha' chapter of the *Adiparva*, there is an erotic description of a bacchanal picnic in which Krishna and Arjuna enjoy in the Khandava forest on the bank of River Yamuna with women, whose hips are heavy and breasts full and who move with an uncertain gait due to heavy drinking. They dance, sing, play on musical instruments and indulge in water sports in the Yamuna waters. Royal women like Draupadi and Subhadra too become tipsy, *madotkata* due to drinking.

The epic also contains the story of Bhangaswana who is born as a man but becomes a woman due to certain circumstances. When Indra asks Bhangaswana if he wants to be man again, the latter refuses by saying that it is the woman who derives greater sexual pleasure during intercourse than man. And yet at another place, it is said that deriving unique sexual pleasure during "*krida, rati* and *vihara*, the demonesses, *danava*-women dress as men and men as women and enjoy each other's company."

Harivamsha is considered an appendix of the *Mahabharata*. Apart from a couple of love stories, there is a very elaborate and erotic description of a picnic where Krishna, Balarama and the Yadavas with their women enjoy at Pindaraka *tirtha* on the sea-shore near Dwaraka. Singing, dancing, music and amorous sports of various kinds constitute an integral part of the orgy at Pindaraka.

It seems to have become a literary trend to describe orgiastic picnics with relish and a lot of eroticism thrown in. In the *Bhagavata Purana,* there is a description of a picnic where Balarama frolics with cowherd girls who are fair as *champak* flowers. Once Balarama returns from Dwaraka to Brindavana to meet his childhood friends. He remains in Braj for two months of *Vasanta ritu* — *Chaitra* and *Vaishaka*. He spends his fragrant nights on the bank of River Yamuna, engaging the cowherd girls in amorous sports. Completely drunk, one night he desires to enjoy water-sports. Under the influence of a heavenly nectar, *varuni,* he orders River Yamuna to change her course and flow near the place where he is picnicking with the cowherd girls. Yamuna simply ignores him. An angry Balarama threatens the Yamuna that he would drag her to him with his plough if she continues to disobey him. A frightened Yamuna, says the *Purana,* changes her course and starts flowing near the spot where Balarama was camping. Balarama then engages the cowherd girls in amorous water-sports.

Balarama has been worshipped in Mathura, Varanasi and Gwalior region since ancient times. His images of the Sunga period have been found in this region. His cult became popular in the Kushana period. A number of his images show him holding, in one hand, a cup of wine while a snake spreads its hood over his head. In Baldeogaon near Mathura is situated a temple of Balarama where worshippers offer him intoxicating cannabis, *bhang*. The most boisterous Holi of Braj region is held every year in the premises of the Balarama temple where women beat men with cloth whips. In the Braj region, there is a place called Ramghat. According to local legend, it is here that Balarama made Yamuna change her course so that he could engage with cowherd girls in amorous water-sports. Here a temple of Balarama has been built at that spot.

After the *Mahabharata,* it was the Buddhist scholar-and-poet, Ashvaghosha, who wrote two beautiful epics, the *Buddhacharita* and *Saundarananda,* in the first century AD. In *Saundarananda,* he describes himself as the son of Suvarnakshi, a resident of Saket — Ayodhya — *bhikshoracharya bhadanta ashvaghosha mahavadin.* He is a contemporary of King Kanishka and is said to have been present in the fourth Buddhist council convened by him. However, his status as a much-revered Buddhist monk does not deter him from writing erotic poetry.

Saundarananda is the story of the Buddha's brother, Nanda, and his exceptionally beautiful wife Sundari. Ashvaghosha has written one full *sarga* describing quite explicitly the amorous sports, including love-making indulged in by Nanda and Sundari. Similarly, Ashvaghosha in *Buddhacharita* depicts the amorous atmosphere prevailing in the harem of Prince Siddhartha. The beautiful women of the royal harem are described as *kamashrayapandita* and *ratikarkasha,* implying that they were experts in amorous sports besides being tough and wild in love-making. With their artful coquetry and provocative flirting, they try to arouse the prince. One woman, on the pretext of being drunk, makes clothes slip from her lovely body again and again; one tries to show him her firm and full buttocks through her diaphanous garment held by a golden *mekhala*; another, on the pretext of telling him some secret in his ear, kisses him on the cheeks; some inebriated women touch him with their full bosoms and some hold him firm in their arms. One of them holds the branch of a mango tree to show him her breasts like pitchers of gold. Such lovely women are sculpted on the railings of the *stupa* found during excavation at the Bhutesar mound in Mathura. A sculpture of a woman holding a branch of a mango tree and provocatively exposing her lovely breasts is found adorning the eastern gate of the Sanchi *stupa*.

Around the same time, under the Satavahanas of Perathisthan in Maharashtra, two great works which were sparkling gems of Indian love literature, emerged on the scene. Interestingly, both were not in Sanskrit as usually all earlier literature was. One of them was in Maharashtri Prakrit and another in an unheard of Paishachi language. It was Gunadhya who wrote his work *Brihatkatha* in Paishachi language. Speaking about the work and its author, Kuvalayamala says that the work is a great book of stories, *vaddakatha*. It further says:

> What is *Brihatkatha*? It is Saraswati, goddess of learning, herself. And Gunadhya is Brahma himself. It is a mine, a treasure of all arts, *sakalakalagamanilaya*; poets become literate after reading it.

This work, written during the rule of a Satavahana king in the first century AD, is lost to posterity. However, its Sanskrit versions, the *Brihatkathashlokasangraha* by Budhaswami and the *Kathasaritsagara* by Somadeva, *Brihatkathamanjiri* of Kshemendra and *Vasudevahindi* by Sanghadasagani are available. Originally, the work was known as a collection of love stories and indeed in the Sanskrit versions, a major portion is dedicated to the love stories of King Udana of Vatsa country and his son, Naravahanadatta. In Jain *Vasudevahindi*, the hero is Vasudeva, father of Krishna, and his love adventures constitute the theme of the work.

The unique collection of over seven hundred love lyrics in Maharashtri Prakrit compiled by King Hala depicts styles of love-making by folk heroes and heroines in different situations.

It seems that the early theatrical entertainments were full of a strong erotic element. The earliest sculpture of a dancer belonging to the Indus Valley era is not only nude but very provocative too in her stance.

Because of all these erotic displays, the Buddha prohibited his disciples from attending dramatic performances by saying that "they induce sensual, misanthropic or mentally confused states in the viewers." Even the law-giver Manu in his *Smriti* prohibits students from watching dramatic shows.

But some Buddhist monks went to the extent of visiting the theatre and inviting female dancers to come and dance on the robes they had spread before them. They were, of course, expelled from the order, the Sangha.

The erotic contents of the popular amusements were so strong that Kautilya in the fourth century BC laid down the rule that "actors may at will entertain the audiences but they must desist from talking about or cracking jokes about copulation betweeen men and women." Magistrates were empowered to punish the breakers of this rule with a fine or severe lashing.

Bharata in his *Natyashastra* tries to curb the tendency of showing amorous activities on the stage by evolving a code of moral conduct for actors. He says:

> As the drama is to be witnessed by the father and the son, the mother-in-law and daughter-in-law, all sitting together, certain acts should be avoided. Women should not be shown as very scantily dressed, wearing only a one-piece garment. They should not be shown on the stage taking a bath, decorating the body, combing their hair or ascending the bed-stead. Sleeping on the stage should not be shown. If out of necessity somebody sleeps alone or with anyone, no kiss or embrace or any private acts such as biting, scratching with nails, loosening of the knot of the garments, the pressing of the breasts and the lips should not be presented on the stage.

It seems from this that short of showing sexual intercourse, every other sexual act was shown during popular dramatic performances.

Now, coming to dramatic literature, we may say that love and romance constituted its core. Dramas were written to depict love stories. In the Gupta period and subsequently many one-act, one-actor *bhana* plays with overt erotic contents were written to depict the lives of courtesans. Barring a very few, the satires, *prahasanas* went beyond, remaining erotic and obscene.

Kalidasa's contribution to erotic literature was in the form of poetic works that he penned.

Ritusamhara is frankly an erotic poem by Kalidasa as it describes in detail the amorous dalliance between lovers in different seasons of the year. His romantic poem *Meghadoota* has its moments of abject eroticism. In the *Kumarsambhava*, he describes *sambhoga sringara* of Shiva and Parvati without any inhibition.

In his *Raghuvamsha,* there is a full chapter on romantic affairs of King Agnivarna, who is extremely fond of making love to beautiful women. He would dress according to the season, visit drinking dens with women to drink wine and make love to them in different postures. For love-making and entertainment, he preferred the lovely dancing girls. Satiated with one, he would seek a new one. Hence, some clever women would get up in the middle of intercourse with him, so that he would not be fully gratified with them and continue to invite them again and again. Kalidasa mentions a love-posture or *asana* named Kanthasutra in which the woman rides astride her lover or sleeps over her lover, slowly and gradually thumping his chest with her full breasts before firmly embracing him. This *asana* is not mentioned in the *Kamasutra* though its more advanced variant, *viparitarati*, is described in it.

After Kalidasa, a number of medieval poets wrote completely erotic poems. The *Gita Govinda* of Jayadeva and *Sringarashataka* by Bhartrihari are the prominent ones among them. However, the most enchanting one is *Chourapanchasika* by the eleventh-century poet, Bilhana.

A poet was appointed to teach a princess who was young and beautiful. Secretly, they established a love relationship. When the king came to know that his daughter was involved with the poet, he, in anger, awarded the death sentence upon the poet. When being taken to the gallows, the poet continued to sing about his love in fifty verses. Seeing the profound love of the poet for his daughter, the king granted him pardon and subsequently, they were allowed to marry.

According to one version, the princess was none else but Chandralekha, daughter of King Veerasinha of Mahilapattana, but according to another, she was Yamini Purnatilaka, daughter of King Madanabhirama of Panchala.

The poem is a lyrical description of a young girl in love, *nayika* before, during and after love-making. Some critics opine, "The poem often degenerates into licence." However, some consider it to be better than the *Meghadoota* of Kalidasa.

The poet describes the *nayika* as *surata-tandava-sutradhari* or stringholder of the wild dance of love-making. She is fond of drinking and *viparitarata.* She is an expert in postures, *bandhas* of *Kamasutra* and is very beautiful. *Chourapanchasika* excels in erotic love-poems of India.

Chapter Seven

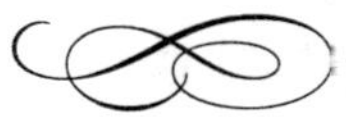

Tales of Love

The twin themes of love and war dominate ancient literature, particularly the epic poetry. However, religious literature and books of hymns contain their share of stories of love interspersed with war. The most ancient work of collection of hymns in India is the *Rig Veda*. In this unique work, there are certain dialogues as also monologues with a pronounced story element. They were known as the *Akhyana suktas* or *Samvada suktas*.

Two such *suktas* are of interest to us. One tells the story of love between King Pururava and a heavenly nymph Urvashi, while the other one is about Yama, the first ancestor, and his sister Yami. Interestingly, both the stories of ancient times revolve around the theme of frustrated love and a tragic end.

In the first story is depicted a lovelorn man who tries to win over his beloved who has deserted him, but he fails. The second story is about a passionate sister who tries to seduce her own brother to cohabit with him but fails again. We do not know why the Vedic seers sang of unfulfilled love or tragic tales of lovers. Did they want to suggest that love always ends in a disaster?

Not much information about Pururava, son of Ila, is found in the *Rig Veda*. Puranic literature calls him a king with his capital at Prathisthana or Prayag. It was he who founded the Somavamsha dynasty. Probably he belonged to the Himalayan region which must have been part of his kingdom. According to the *Shatapatha Brahmana,* Urvashi finds him roaming in the Kurukshetra region of which he might have been the king.

Writing about this class of nymphs, *apsaras,* in his *Vedic Mythology*, Macdonell says that the oldest concept of *apsaras* is that of celestial water-nymphs who are consorts of demi-gods, the *gandharvas*. They are spoken of as residing on certain trees. *Gandharvas* and *apsaras* on such trees are considered propitious to any passing wedding procession. They are engaged in dance, song and play. The *Atharva Veda* says that they are fond of playing dice and bestow luck at play, but are feared, especially for causing mental derangement. Magic is therefore employed against them.

The Urvashi myth too grew with the growth of epics and the *Puranas*. However, the *Rig Veda*, in which her love story occurs, does not give us much information about this beautiful *apsara*, except for saying that Sage Vashistha was born to her and that she is invoked with streams.

The full context of the love story between Urvashi and Pururava is given by the *Shatapatha Brahmana,* in which the lovers get united. But, the *Rig Veda* does not speak of their union and the story culminates in a tragedy. According to *Shatapatha Brahmana,* Urvashi deserts her mortal lover Pururava and "passed away from him like the firsts of the dawns" becoming "hard to catch like the winds". One day, she appears before him and he implores her to stay back stating that he had lost his prowess when she deserted him and become so weak that he now could not take out the arrow from the quiver for glory. He even threatens her with suicide.

Urvashi tells him that he is born to protect the earth as a king and should not think of self-annihilation but continue doing his duty. She further states that "a female friendship does not exist; their hearts are the hearts of jackals."

With this advice, Urvashi departs from him. The parting shot is that they may unite in heaven after his death!

Thus ends the first love story of mankind in abject tragedy. Several versions of this Vedic story with a happy ending are found in later literature but they lack the substance and sheer grit of the original. The independent, self-willed Urvashi of the *Rig Veda* gives way to a weak, love-lorn, submissive shadow of the original in later literature, particularly in Kalidasa's play *Vikramorvashiya.*

Same is the case with the Yama-Yami story, again found in the *Rig Veda* in a form of dialogue. Yama is considered as the first ancestor of mankind, "the first father of mankind and the first to die", and of later becoming the god of death. Yami is his twin sister who implores him to cohabit with her for continuation of the human race.

Yama rejects the advances of his twin sister on moral grounds and asks her to find joy in somebody else's embrace. Thus, the second love story of the *Rig Veda* too ends tragically for the beloved.

In Vatsyayana's famous treatise on love, the *Kamasutra,* he says that the girl to be seduced should be told love stories of different kinds to help her make up her mind for embarking on love adventures. The types of stories he narrates are stories of lovers meeting secretly by cheating other people around, *kapata akhyana;* folk stories of love, *lokavrittanta;* romantic stories, *kavikatha* written by poets; stories of how men procured wives of other men, *paradarikakatha.*

Vatsyayana further says that love stories like those of Ahalya, Avimaraka and Shakuntala should be told to encourage the girl to establish her relationships with her lover boldly. The story of Ahalya and her adulterous affair with Indra, the king of gods, is given in Vedic literature. Here, Indra is addressed as the paramour of Ahalya. Different versions of the Ahalya-Indra romance are found in the epics and the *Puranas.*

Ahalya was born from the mind of Brahma, *manas-kanya.* She was extremely beautiful and many gods wanted to marry her, but Brahma gave her to Sage Sharadwata Gautama. After marriage, she went to live on the Brahmagiri mountain.

One day, Indra, assuming the guise of Sage Gautama, goes to his hermitage. Seeing that the sage is not around, he approaches the young and beautiful Ahalya and expresses his desire to cohabit with her. Despite his clever disguise, Ahalya recognises Indra. Out of curosity to study the king of gods intimately, she gives her consent. His love-making gives her immense pleasure. Expressing her satisfaction, she asks him to leave soon and save her from the wrath of her husband.

Meanwhile, Indra continues to visit her. One day, Gautama's pupils point out to Sage Gautama, the other sage sitting with Ahalya. Indra tries to escape by assuming the form of a cat. But Gautama recognises him. The angry sage punishes him and his own wife by cursing them.

The moral of the story, as implied by Vatsyayana, is that Ahalya boldly accepts Indra and enjoys his company without bothering about the wrath of her husband. This is the way of love.

It seems the story of Shakuntala was known to Vedic literature though a full exposition is found in the epic *Mahabharata*.

In the *Shatapatha Brahmana*, Shakuntala is described as an *apsara* who gives birth to Bharata on the bank of River Nadpat. Bharata too is referred to as Dushyanti Bharata or son of Dushyanta who had performed many *ashvamedha yajnas*.

However, the love story of Dushyanta and Shakuntala is for the first time mentioned elaborately in the *Mahabharata* when Shakuntala carries Dushyanta's love-child.

Once Maharshi Vishvamitra takes to observing severe austerities which make Indra, the king of heaven, apprehensive. He thinks that on the completion of his *tapas*, Vishvamitra would become more powerful than him. Hence, Indra deputes a very beautiful *apsara*, named Menaka, to seduce him and break his *tapas*.

The lovely Menaka goes near the hermitage of Vishvamitra and starts fooling around playfully. Suddenly a strong gust of wind blows away her moon-like sparkling clothes. Feigning shyness, she runs after her clothes, stark naked. Vishvamitra sees the young and extremely beautiful maiden running naked in exasperation.

Vishvamitra's carnal instincts get aroused at the sight of a nude *apsara* and he falls for her. For a long period, they spend their time in making love to each other.

Menaka becomes pregnant. One day, she gives birth to a

daughter on the bank of River Malini flowing through the Himalayan region. She then abandons her newborn daughter and leaves for heaven.

The *Shakunta* birds look after her and give her protection from the forest animals. Kanva Muni finds her and takes her to his hermitage where she grows into a very beautiful girl.

One day, King Dushyanta, son of Ilila, goes to the forest on a hunting expedition. When he comes to know that the hermitage of Kanva Muni is nearby, he enters it, leaving behind his army.

He finds that Kanva is not in his hermitage. When Dushyanta calls out to find out if anybody is around, Shakuntala comes forward and receives him. Stunned by her beauty, he offers to make her his queen. Shakuntala tells him that she would accept him on the condition that the son born to her would be the heir to his throne. When the king agrees, Shakuntala enters into a physical relationship with him without the prior permission of her father Kanva.

The *Kamasutra* states that the story of Shakuntala, who did not seek her father's permission before entering into love, would inspire the young girls to ignore their elders and enjoy the company of their lovers.

Kalidasa wrote two plays on the love stories of Shakuntala and Urvashi with some twist.

Yashodhara, the commentator on *Kamasutra*, mentions another love story in this context — the love story of the moon-god Chandra and Tara, wife of his preceptor Brihaspati. A number of versions of this story are found in different *Puranic* works.

Brihaspati, the preceptor of gods, has a very beautiful wife named Tara. Enamoured by the handsome moon-god, Chandra, she elopes with him and starts living with him. Brihaspati tries his best to regain his wife but she refuses to go back to him. When Brihaspati finally approaches Indra, the angry king of gods declares war on Chandra. Shukracharya, the preceptor of demons, is an old enemy of Brihaspati and so joins hands with Chandra. A regular war between the gods and demons ensues. Ultimately, Brahma intervenes and makes Chandra return Tara to Brihaspati.

The titillating love story of Tara and Chandra became so popular that, according to *Naishadhiyacharita*, a four-act play in *natika* form and based on it was written and enacted. The basis of this *natika* was an erotic feeling born out of love, *smarodbhutabhava*. Defining the characteristics of the *Natika Bharata,* in his *Natya Shastra,* he says that it should contain dances, songs, recitation and amorous sports — *bahunrittagi tapathya ratisambhogatmika.*

Yashodhara implies that this story should be so told as to dissuade women from leaving their husbands for their lovers.

The love story of Avimaraka, as mentioned by Vatsyayana, is not found in classical literature. Probably it was playwright Bhasa who imagined and depicted it through the play, *Avimaraka.* This is a love story of a handsome youth, who is a low-caste Chandala in the country of King Kuntibhoja and of Kurangi, who is the daughter of King Kuntibhoja. Avimaraka is smuggled into the king's harem and he sexually enjoys the company of Princess Kurangi for several days. The moral of the story, according to Vatsyayana, is that young girls without any hesitation secretly bring in their lovers to their homes and enjoy their company.

A near similar love story of Usha, daughter of Banasura, who is the king of Shonitpura and of Aniruddha, who is the grandson of Krishna, prince of Dwaraka, is found in the *Puranas.*

Once Usha sees an extremely handsome youth making love to her in her dream. Her friend Chitralekha draws the paintings of many young men of the time and Usha identifies Aniruddha, as the lover in her dreams, from among them. Chitralekha, with her *yogic* powers, flies down to Dwaraka and brings the sleeping Aniruddha back to Usha in Shonitpura. Aniruddha remains concealed in the harem for a long time, making love to Usha. One day, Banasura's guards catch and arrest him. An angry Krishna attacks Shonitpura, defeats Banasura and brings back Usha and Aniruddha to Dwaraka.

Thus, love and war form the core of many ancient love stories. Rukmini, the princess of Vidarbha, writes a love letter to Krishna. Krishna reaches Kundinpura, the capital of Vidarbha, and while Rukmini is returning after worshipping Amba in her temple, he lifts her up in his chariot and speeds away. Prince Rukmi, who was opposed to their alliance, pursues Krishna with his army. In the war that ensues, Krishna defeats him.

Once, while Arjuna is camping in Dwaraka, he sees Krishna's young and beautiful sister Subhadra during a grand festival organised on a mountain, Raivataka. Krishna tells the love-smitten Arjuna that Kshatriyas organise *swayamvaras* to marry off their daughters. "But, you can never trust the nature of women because in a *swayamvara*, Subhadra may not choose Arjuna." Hence, he asks Arjuna to simply kidnap her. Arjuna does exactly that and carries away Subhadra in his chariot. Krishna pacifies the angry Yadavas and war is averted.

In the love story of Usha and Aniruddha, the element of magic is introduced in the form of Chitralekha flying through air and carrying a sleeping Aniruddha to Usha in Shonitpura. Similarly the element of magic forms part of many ancient love stories.

A story of a Brahmin youth is found in Somadeva's work, *Kathasaritsagara*, which is based on an ancient story, *Brihatkatha*, written in Paishachi language and ascribed to first or second century AD.

In the city of Varanasi, there lived a young and handsome Brahmin named Somadatta. He was the son of a pious Brahmin named Chandraswami. In the same city lived Srigarbha, the beautiful daughter of a businessman. His other daughter Bandhudatta was married to the chief trader of Mathura and who was named Varahadatta. On a visit to her father's house in Varanasi, Bandhutatta one day sees Somadatta through the window of her house. She instantly falls in love with the Brahmin youth. Somadatta and Bandhudatta begin meeting secretly in the house of a female friend of the latter to make love.

One day, Bandhudatta's husband returns from Mathura to take her home. She becomes sad at the prospect of separation from her lover. She goes to a *yogini* named Sukhashaya for advice. She gives Bandhudatta a magic thread and tells her that on tying the thread around the neck of her lover, he would turn into a monkey and on untying it, he would become a human again. Thus, she would be able to take her lover to Mathura in the form of a monkey.

Whenever she desired to make love to him, she could untie the thread. Her husband does not object to her taking a pet monkey to Mathura. And the affair continues till Somadatta escapes from the clutches of Bandhudatta.

In the same work, there are stories of men who love witches and suffer severe consequences. In the city of Varanasi, there lived a young man named Nishchayadatta. He comes in contact with a *gupta yogini* or a Brahmin beauty practicing witchcraft. They become lovers. Her name is Somada. Once Nishchayadatta, out of jealousy, gives her a sound beating. She quietly tolerates it, but the next day, when she gets an opportunity, she ties a magic thread around his neck and turns him into a bull. She then sells him to a trader who uses him for carting merchandise.

In the same work we find stories of young men, who reject the love of witches and suffer for it. There are stories of men who are loved by semi-divine women like *yakshis*, *vidyadharis* and *apsaras*.

In literary works, we find several stories of courtesans' love. In most cases, the men are duped but there are also stories of *ganikas* who love their men intensely, not for their money but for their good qualities of head and heart. They remain faithful to them till the end of their lives. The most famous among them is the *ganika* Vasantasena of Ujjayani who loved a poor but handsome Brahmin businessman, Charudatta. Playwrights Bhasa and after him Shudraka have written beautiful plays, *Charudatta* and *Mricchakatika* respectively, based on their love.

In a story, Kacha was a young and handsome son of Brihaspati, the preceptor of gods. Kaviputra Shukracharya was the preceptor of *asuras* and knew the knowledge, *vidya* of bringing back the dead to life (known as *mrita sanjivani vidya*). Brihaspati sends Kacha to Shukracharya to learn this *vidya*. Shukracharya lays down the condition that he would have to teach the guru's daughter Devayani's son the unique *vidya* that he possesses. Kacha agrees and Shukracharya willingly accepts Kacha as his disciple. Kacha takes the vow of celibacy as was necessary in those days and starts serving the guru and his lovely daughter. Kacha pleases the guru with his scholarship and erudition and the daughter with singing, dancing and playing on musical instruments.

In course of time, young Devayani becomes fond of Kacha. She remains near him and entertains him with sweet music. The infuriated *danavas* twice kill Kacha but Shukracharya brings him back to life by using his powers. The third time they kill Kacha and burn him to ash. Then mixing his ash into wine, they offer it to Shukracharya, who is immensely fond of drinking.

The third time, Shukracharya uses his *vidya* and calls out to Kacha, who replies from the stomach of his guru and tells him all that has happened. The guru asks him to stay put and teaches him the *mrita sanjivani vidya*. This brings Kacha to life and he emerges, tearing the stomach of his guru. After coming out, he restores his guru to life by using his newly acquired knowledge.

With his mission accomplished, Kacha seeks his guru's permission to return to his father. A lovelorn Devayani pleads that he should marry her. But Kacha refuses by saying that like her, he too had been born from Shukracharya and in his new incarnation, he is unable to accept her as now she is his sister, that is siblings of the same father. An angry Devayani curses Kacha but her love life is destroyed.

This tragic story of betrayal does not end here. She later marries King Yayati. Sharmishtha, daughter of the *danava* king, Vrishparva, too goes with Devayani as her maid as she had been meted out a punishment for her past deeds. Sharmishtha is very beautiful. She seduces King Yayati and makes him her secret lover. This second betrayal shatters Devayani completely.

Apart from love stories of Shakuntala and Damayanti, there are a number of love stories in the epic, *Mahabharata*. No wonder, apart from calling the epic an *Arthashastra* and *Dharmashastra*, it is called *Kamashastra* also — *Kamashastramidam proktam Vyasenamita-buddhina*.

The composer of the epic, Maharshi Vyasa, himself was a love-child by birth. Once Muni Parashara sees a very young and beautiful fisherwoman of dark complexion named Satyavati on the bank of River Yamuna. As she smells of fish, she acquires fame as *matsyagandha*. She had a beautiful smile, her thighs were like stems of the banana plant and she was excessively pretty. His passions aroused, Muni Parashara expresses his desire to make love to her. Blushing profusely, she asks the Muni to look around and see for himself that both shores of River Yamuna were crowded with people. The Muni with his powers creates a dense fog and in the darkness that envelopes the place, he makes love to Satyavati. The pleased Muni grants her a boon that her body henceforth would emit lovely fragrance and she would come to be known as *yojanagandha*.

Satyavati gives birth to Vyasa on an island in the Yamuna river; hence he comes to be known as *dwaipayana,* one born on a *dwipa,* island.

King Shantanu of Hastinapura once sees Satyavati on the bank of River Yamuna. He gets so smitten by her beauty that he approaches her fisherman-father to seek her hand in marriage. The father places the condition that the son born to her should be made the heir to his kingdom; the king agrees. Bhishma, Shantanu's son from Ganga, agrees to forego his claim to the throne of Hastinapura and promises Dasharaja that the son born to his daughter Satyavati would become the king after Shantanu.

The two love stories of Yojanagandha and Satyavati are very famous in the epic *Mahabharata*. The other equally famous love story of the epic is that of Kacha and Devayani.

Love stories abound in Vedic literature, epics and *Puranas* as also in the sectarian works of Jains, Buddhists, etc. But it was Gunadhya, who during the reign of Satavahana kings, around first or second century AD, compiled a book comprising exclusively of love stories in Paishachi language under the title *Brihatkatha*. Bhana describes it as *Samuddipitakandarpa Brihatkatha*. Hence, Dr Vasudevasarana Agarwal assumes that the original nature of this collection was of love stories, *kama kathas*. The original work is lost to posterity, but its Sanskrit versions, such as *Brihatkathashlokasangraha* by Budhaswami, *Brihatkathamanjiri* by

Kshemendra, and *Kathasaritsagara* by Somadevabhatta are available. Its Prakrit version in Jain tradition, *Vasudevahindi*, was written by Sanghadasagani.

It is believed that the original *Brihatkatha* contained the Udayana series of stories. Apart from the love adventures of King Udayana, it contained love tales of his son, Naravahanadatta.

Of all the love tales in these works, the most famous one is of Udayana and Vasavadatta. The Mathura Museum has a sculpture showing Udayana eloping with Vasavadatta, astride an elephant. It is ascribed to second century BC. In his poem *Meghadoota,* Kalidasa says that in the city of Avanti and the villages around, there were many old men who were adept in narrating the Udayana story—*Udayankathakovidagramavriddha.* They narrate how Udayana, the young and handsome King of Vatsa elopes with the darling daughter of King Pradyota of Ujjayani. Then, they point to the forest of *tal* trees, in the *talavana,* planted by the king and how the elephant Nalagiri roams about in rut, by freeing himself from the peg he was tied to.

The debonair king leaves the administration of his kingdom to his able ministers like Yaugandharayana and Rukmanvan. He is expert in playing on his *veena* named Ghoshavati. His hobby is to lure elephants by playing music on his Ghoshavati and capture them.

During the same period, there lives Chandamahasena, a powerful king of Ujjayani. He has a very beautiful daughter, Vasavadatta by name. The king thinks that if Udayana were to teach the musical instrument, *veena* to his daughter, not only would he come in contact with her and eventually fall in love with her but gradually become his son-in-law too.

Accordingly, through a messenger, King Chandamahasena asks Vatsaraj to come to Ujjayani and teach the *veena* to his daughter. This angers Udayana and he sends a reply saying that if the princess of Ujjayani wants to learn the musical instrument, she would have to come to Kaushambi.

King Chandamahasena then decides to capture Udayana deceitfully and bring him to Ujjayani. He makes an exact replica of his famous elephant Nalagiri and in his stomach conceals a battalion of soldiers. Then he gets this mechanical elephant, *yantra-hasti*, placed in the dense forest of Vindyachala.

Udayana, on coming to know about the elephant, decides to capture it. He leaves his soliders behind and ventures out alone to the forest, playing on his *veena* to mesmerise the elephant with its music. As soon as he draws near the elephant, the soldiers of Chandamahasena emerge from its stomach and capture Udayana to take him captive to Ujjayani.

There, on the request of Chandamahasena, he agrees to teach the *veena* to his daughter Vasavadatta. As soon as Udayana sees her, he falls in love with her. Gradually, Vasavadatta too starts loving him. Meanwhile ministers of Udayana reach Ujjayani. They help the king to elope with his royal disciple Vasavadatta, astride her elephant Bhadravati.

King Chandamahasena does not mind this and sends his son, Gopalak, to Kaushambi to marry off princess Vasavadatta to King Udayana with fanfare.

Playwright Bhasa, in fourth century BC, wrote two plays — *Pratijna Yaugandharayana* and *Swapnavasavadatta*, depicting the Udayana stories.

Swapnavasavadatta is considered as one of the best plays in Sanskrit dramatic literature. It speaks of the profound love of Vasavadatta for which she makes many sacrifices.

Sanskrit dramatic literature is replete with love stories. However, one of the rather erotic plays is *Malati Madhava*, written by poet Bhavabhuti in the eighth century. In the prologue of the play, he states that knowledge of the *Kamasutra* is essential for writing the play. *Malati Madhava* betrays a profound influence of *Kamasutra*. In the play, the sleeping heroine, Malati, shows all physical signs of having intercourse with her lover in her dream, right on the stage. It is stated in *Mricchakatika* of Shudraka that young courtesans were required to read dramas full of romance and eroticism — *Natyam pathyante sasringaram*. The dramatic forms, known as *bhana* and *prahasana*, are quite erotic and deal with the love stories of courtesans.

In works like *Kathasaritsagara,* based on the ancient classic *Brihatkatha,* we find a number of stories that carry a touch of humour or are outright humorous. One such humorous love story, found in Vishnusharma's *Panchatantra,* is given below:

In a certain city there lived two young friends, Kaulika and a charioteer, *rathakara.* Once they go to attend a festival of some deity in the neighbouring city. In the crowd of people, they come across a very beautiful princess riding an elephant guarded by soldiers. On seeing her, Kaulika is struck by the arrow of Cupid. Becoming unconscious, he falls to the ground.

A worried *rathakara* takes him home and after receiving treatment, Kaulika regains his consciousness. After much persuasion, Kaulika tells his friend that he is sure to die of love pangs and that nobody on earth would be able to save him. And the cause of his love-sickness is none else but the beautiful princess astride the elephant.

The *rathakara* laughs out aloud. He asks his friend Kaulika to stop worrying and get ready to unite with her that very night itself.

Kaulika asks his friend why he is playing the fool with him, because who could think of entering the king's harem that was heavily guarded by soldiers day and night, and be able to enjoy the company of the princess.

Asking his friend to keep patience, *rathakara* carves out a mechanical bird, *garuda* that can fly in the air by manipulating keys attached to it. He fits two additional arms to Kaulika to make him look like Lord Vishnu and thus hide his real identity.

"Now," says the *rathakara,* "you can fly to the seventh floor of the royal palace at midnight and present yourself to the princess as Lord Vishnu himself. When she is impressed by your disguise and clever talk, make love to her according to the techniques devised by Maharshi Vatsyayana in his love-manual, the *Kamasutra.*"

Kaulika does exactly as instructed. When the princess sees "Lord Vishnu" himself standing before her in her bedroom, she is struck dumb. Kaulika tells her that he has come to her by leaving behind Lakshmi, his wife, in the milky ocean, his abode, and now she must make love to him.

Startled at his words, the princess informs him that since she is a mere mortal, how could a mortal make love to a divine?

Kaulika is taken aback but regaining his composure, he grandly tells her that in fact she is not a mere mortal but his consort Radha herself, who has taken birth as a princess.

"In that case," says the princess, "you would need to approach my father who would gladly give me in marriage to you."

Feigning anger, he shouts at her and tells her that a divinity like him cannot simply appear before any one. "If you refuse to make love to me, I will curse your family and burn them to ashes," he threatens. So saying, he takes the frightened and shy girl to bed and enjoys sleeping with her according to the procedures of love-making in Vatsyayana's *Kamasutra*. After that, he starts visiting her every night.

Watching the signs of love-making on her body, her personal maids decide to report the matter to her father, the king.

An angry queen interrogates her daughter and is delighted to learn that every night "Lord Vishnu" visits her daughter. To verify the matter, both the king and the queen conceal themselves in a convenient corner in the palace and behold, at midnight, "Lord Vishnu" arrives astride his *garuda* into the bedroom of their daughter and remains there till morning.

The king is very happy to get "Lord Vishnu" as his son-in-law. Meanwhile, the soldiers of neighbouring countries launch an attack on his land. Through his daughter, every night the king starts sending messages to the fake Vishnu for help in eliminating the enemy.

Finding himself in a peculiar situation, Kaulika at last decides to appear before the enemy which has by now laid siege to the capital. He thinks that maybe on seeing him hover above them in the sky in the guise of Vishnu, the enemy would run away out of fright.

Meanwhile Lord Vishnu calls his mighty bird *garuda* and instructs him that Kaulika in his guise is certain to die at the hands of the enemy and that his mechanical *garuda* would crash to the ground on attack by the enemy's arrows.

The *garuda* laughs and tells his divine master that Kaulika should be made to reap the fruits of his misdeeds.

But an exasperated Lord Vishnu tells the *garuda* that if Kaulika were to be defeated or killed, then, not knowing the reality, the people would presume that the Lord Vishnu himself has been defeated. "In that case, who would worship me in future?"

Now the *garuda* understands the situation. Lord Vishnu asks the *garuda* to enter the body of the fake *garuda* while he himself enters the body of Kaulika to vanquish the enemy forces and save his own reputation. In the battle that ensues, Kaulika defeats his foes easily. The king is extremely happy at Kaulika's valour and offers his daughter, the princess, in marriage to him.

There are a number of love stories of clever adulterous men and women who indulge in joyous love-making without getting caught. They could hoodwink even the gods by their strategy of deceit.

Here is an interesting Jain story of a clever adulteress. In the city of Varanasi there lived a beautiful woman, who was the wife of a rich trader. She had a secret lover with whom she enjoyed the pleasures of life.

The father of the trader comes to know about the extra-marital affair of his daughter-in-law. He becomes very angry and informs his son about the escapades of his wife.

But the wife insists that she is innocent. So it is decided that she should undergo penance in the temple of a local *yaksha,* as it was believed that a person could not pass through the legs of a *yaksha* image without being trapped in his testicles.

The clever woman tells her lover to be present on the way to the temple in the guise of a demon and touch her. She then takes a purifying bath and moves towards the *yaksha* temple. As pre-planned, her lover intercepts her on the journey and touches her.

After that she reaches the *yaksha* temple and stands before his image. She then utters plaintively that the *yaksha* has the right to punish her if she has touched any person other than her husband and the demon who has crossed her path on the way to temple.

Totally baffled, the *yaksha* looks at the woman in front of him in amazement.

Before he can come out of his confusion and act, she quickly passes through his legs without being entrapped. The *yaksha* cannot do anything except to fume with helpless rage because what the woman has told is nothing but the truth.

There are a number of very interesting love stories in which we find women in love communicating with their lovers through a code language or symbols that their male friends could alone decode, understand and act upon. Here is one illustration from a Jain literature:

In the city of Vasantapura, there lived a young and beautiful wife of a rich man. A young man sees her taking a bath in the river.

He says, "The river is asking you whether you have enjoyed your bath or not."

The woman replies: "We shall try our best to please those who ask whether we have enjoyed our bath."

Smitten by her beauty, he tries to find out who she is. He soon discovers that she is the daughter-in-law of a certain trader.

He visits a nun and requests her to carry his love-message to the young beauty. The nun approaches the girl, who is attending to her household chores. The girl becomes terribly angry at being disrupted and with her hand smeared with lamp-black, stamps the mark of five fingers on the nun's back.

The boy understands that the object of his desire has asked her to meet him on the fifth day of the black fortnight. But where? The boy sends the nun again to the house of the trader's beautiful daughter-in-law. This time, the girl hits the nun and throws her into a clump of Ashoka trees by a gap in the fence.

The boy instantly understands that the woman wants to meet him in the clump of Ashoka trees near her house. So the boy goes there on the fifth day of the black fortnight and finds her waiting for him (summary of a story in *The Clever Adulteress*).

Another story of a similar genre but with a different ending can be found in Somadevabhatta's *Kathasaritsagara*. It says:

A young boy named Devadatta reaches the city of Pratishthana and starts staying with an old guru to learn the *Shastras*. One day,

Sri, the beautiful daughter of a local king, Susharma, sees him from the window of her palace and instantly falls in love with him. She beckons to him and as he approaches near, she bites a flower, *pushpa*, with her teeth, *danta*, and throws it at him before disappearing. He is unable to understand the meaning of Sri's action. But suffering the pangs of love, he loses all interest in learning.

The old *acharya* understands that something is amiss. He asks Devadatta why he is looking so forlorn and depressed. After much persuasion, he narrates the story of Sri throwing him a flower bitten by her teeth.

On hearing the story of Devadatta, the clever *acharya* tells him that biting of a flower, *pushpa* with teeth, *danta* means that Sri has invited him to the temple of Pushpa-Danteshvara for a secret meeting.

Delighted by this revelation, Devadatta rushes to the temple and hides himself behind the door. On the day of *Ashtami*, the princess goes alone to the temple without any of her maids. When she sees her lover hiding behind the temple door, she runs and embraces him joyfully.

"How could you decode my message?" asks the princess eagerly.

"Not me; it was my guru who understood your message," replies Devadatta truthfully.

She pushes him away and says, "You are nothing but an illiterate fool."

Afraid that her secret, which the guru already knew, would spread around, she rushes back to the palace.

The epic, *Ramayana* can be described as a tragic love story of Rama, the prince of Ayodhya, and his wife Sita, with suspicion casting its shadow over their lives.

In the *Mahabharata*, the love story of Nala, the king of *Nishadha* country, and Damayanti, daughter of King Bhima of Vidarbha and who suffered for long at the hands of fate, is described in detail. Damayanti falls in love with Nala after hearing from a swan the qualities of the young *Nishadha* king. In her *swayamvara*, five guardian deities, *lokapalas* including Indra disguise themselves to look like Nala and go and stand by his side in the hope of proving the lucky one to marry her. Being clever, the princess is able to spot the real Nala among them and marries him. But subsequently, she has to undergo plenty of hardships before finding happiness.

It is interesting to note that the Vedic piece, *Shatapatha Brahmana,* mentions Nala as *Nada Naishadhi,* meaning one whose enemies fear him. The treatise compares him with Yama, the god of death, because of his capacity to inflict death on his enemies. But there is no trace of this love story in Vedic literature. Later, in the twelfth century AD, the poet, Sri Harsha, wrote his epic poem *Naishadhiyacharita* based on the Nala-Damayanti story.

In *Gatha Saptashati* compiled by Hala Satavahana, for the first time ever reference is made to the great Indian love story of Radha and Krishna. Radha is a beautiful cowherd girl in the pastoral Braj region on the bank of River Yamuna, and which has the ancient city of Mathura as its centre. For the first time, it is in the epic *Mahabharata* that Krishna's story is described in detail. In fact, in the opening line of the very first verse of the epic, salutations are offered to him. A Belva inscription describes him as the *Mahabharata sutradhar.* However, neither in the *Mahabharata* nor in its appendix is Harivamsha Radha mentioned.

Major *Vaishnava Puranas,* like the *Vishnu Purana* and the *Bhagavata Purana,* do not mention Radha's romantic dalliance with Krishna but his frolics with the beautiful cowherd girls find place in them. The *Ras Lila* dance Krishna performs with cowherd girls, who are fair as *champak* flowers, on the full-moon night of *Sharada ritu* on the bank of River Yamuna finds place in the *Puranas,* which do not mention Radha like the *Vishnu Purana, Harivamsha* and the *Bhagavata* do.

Some scholars trace the inclusion of the circular *Ras* dance in the *Vaishnava Puranas* to the tantric tradition. *Ras* is somewhat akin to the *yoginichakra* or the *Bhairava-chakra* in which the *yoginis* dance around Shiva Bhairava. Most of the *yogini* temples, such as the ones at Hirapur, Ranipur-Jharial in Orissa and at Bhedaghat on the bank of River Narmada in Madhya Pradesh originally had central shrines dedicated to Shiva Bhairava. All the *yoginis* in the Ranipur-Jharial circular temple are depicted in beautiful dancing postures.

Description of the *Ras* dance grew more and more erotic with the *Bhagavata Purana* dedicating full five chapters to its description. Culmination of this erotic element is found in the *Bramhavaivarta Purana* which introduces Radha in the *Ras* dance in a big way. It is interesting to note that in the *Yogini Tantra*, the word *'raskrida'* is used in the sense of sexual intercourse.

Some scholars like Chandrabali Pandey trace the origin of Radha to the tantric tradition. According to them, initially Radhika had no link with the life of Krishna. She was the product of Buddhist *tantra sadhana*. According to the Buddhist *Grihyasamaja Tantra* for conducting *vidyavrata* rituals, it was necessary to take a sixteen-year old girl as a partner. She was called *Sadhika* or *Radhika*. Later she entered the life of Krishna as his beloved, *parakiya nayika*. In the medieval tantric Vaishnava Sahajiya cult, Radha again manifests herself in her tantric form. As Sashibhusan Dasgupta, famous author of *An Introduction to Tantric Buddhism*, has said:

> The *sahaja sadhana* of Vaishnavas grew mainly with the philosophy of Radha and Krishna and their eternal love in the land of eternity.

But in poetry, right from the *Gatha Saptashati*, Radha appears to be the *nayika* than a mere female companion in *tantric sadhana*. It was the twelfth-century poet Jayadeva who portrayed Radha as *nayika* in his beautiful poetic composition, the *Gita Govinda*, mostly following the *nayika-bheda* described in the *Natya Shastra* of Bharata. With *Gita Govinda*, Radha gained prominence in Indian literature. The love-religion, as propounded by Jayadeva, has been taken to greater heights by poets like Vidyapati and Chandidasa of Bengal, by Surdas and numerous others of Braj and by Meera of Rajasthan. Practically in every part of country, the love poetry centering round Krishna and Radha flourished. It influenced other arts like dance, drama, music and painting.

Jayadeva intended his *Gita Govinda* to be erotic. In the opening song itself, he clearly says that the poem is for those who are interested in the fine art of amorous sports of Lord Krishna, *vilaskala*.

He goes to the extent of describing *viparitarata* involving Radha and Krishna. By all standards, the *Gita Govinda* is the greatest and the best love-poem of the world with Radha and Krishna, being the supreme love pair.

The *Vaishnava* Sahajiyas gave a new dimension to the Radha-Krishna love. Explaining this, Dasgupta says that all men and women were considered as physical manifestations of the principles of Radha and Krishna. So the highest state of union between the two sexes, which is the state of supreme love, is the final state of *sahaja*.

Another offshoot of the same thinking is the concept of *parakiya prema*. *Parakiya* means belonging to another. Radha was *parakiya* in the sense that she was the wife of another cowherd. Hence, the conclusion that *parakiya prema* is the highest form of love. This was similar to Shiva-Shakti of the Hindu *tantras* or Prajna and Upaya of Buddhist *tantras*.

Another great pair of lovers was that of the great ascetic Shiva and Parvati, the beautiful daughter of the Himalayas. Their love is depicted in a number of *Puranas* but finds a highly romantic and somewhat erotic expression in Kalidasa's *Kumarasambhava*:

> The *kapalika's* ideal of salvation was to become like Shiva and enjoy the pleasures of love with a consort as beautiful as Parvati (says Desai).

Seldom do we come across a ribald story in ancient Indian literature. One such tale is found in the collection of Buddhist *Jatakas* under the title *Nalinika Jataka*. It is a story of a boy-ascetic who has not seen a woman in his entire life. His name is Rishi Sringa or the 'unicorn sage'. Princess Nalinika, daughter of King Bhahmadatta of Varanasi, is deputed to seduce him. When he sees her, a female, then out of fright, he hides himself in his hut. Curiously, when he looks out again, he sees her playing with a ball, exposing her beautiful limbs, even her procreative organ.

Gathering courage, he invites her inside his hut. When she sits before him, she exposes herself to him in such a way that he sees her procreative organ. She explains that particular part of her anatomy by concocting a clever story and makes him perform intercourse with her.

When his father returns to the hermitage, he describes about her to him in a most funny manner, bordering on ribaldry at places. The father realises what has happened and asks him to keep away from such dangerous creatures in future.

Milder versions of this story are found in the *Ramayana* and the *Mahabharata*.

There are a number of works of later period with erotic content, like *Amaru Shataka, Chaurapanchasika* or Bhartrihari's *Sringarashataka*.

In dramatic literature we find some ribald plays known as *prahasanas* — they are humorous but rather obscene.

Chapter Eight

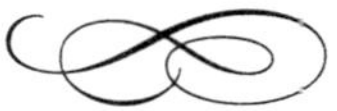

Practice of Love

King Agnivarna of Kalidasa's epic poem, *Raghuvamsha* believed in taking only two things on his lap — one, the musical instrument, *veena*, and the other, a beautiful young woman. What is common between the two?

The *Kamasutra* says that a woman is just like a musical instrument. Man must know the art and technique of playing on both, if he desires to create good music or the music of love. In the case of the latter, the ancient Indians believed in gradually building up the tempo, that is, the speed and rhythm in the feeling of love. For that they suggested many ways to reach the climax and have recorded them in numerous *Kamasutras*, the most prominent among them being the *Kamasutra* of Vatsyayana, which takes note of previous works and traditions of masters, *acharyas* in the field.

Nagarasarvasva says that a girl upto the age of sixteen is called *bala*; till thirty, she is *taruni*; she is *abhirudha* or *praudha* between thirty to fifty and after fifty, she becomes *vriddha*, unfit for the festival of love. A *bala* is fit to be enjoyed in *Grishma ritu* and in *Sharada*, a *taruni* in *Hemanta* and *Shishira*, a *praudha* in *Varsha ritu* and *Vasanta*, and a *vriddha* is to be avoided.

Just as the sixteen phases, *kalas* grow and diminish in *Krishna* and *Shukla Pakshas*, dark and white fortnights, the erotic feelings grow and diminish in the sixteen parts of a girl's body. In the *Shukla*

Paksha, the feeling travels from the toes of the feet to the forehead and during the *Krishna Paksha*, it descends down from the forehead to the toes. Hence, to arouse a woman, the knowledge of this calendar is necessary as her erogenous zones alter according to the position of the moon.

The pre-coitus phase is like the fine-tuning of a musical instrument before playing it.

To fine-tune a girl for better results, it is necessary that she should be brought to a cheerful frame of mind. For that, says Vatsyayana, it is necessary to take her to attend various forms of amusements including festivals, social gatherings, drinking parties and picnics.

Among the festivals which can bring cheer to her mind, Vatsyayana specifically mentions *Yaksharatri, Kaumudi Jagat* and *Suvasantaka*. *Yaksharatri* is akin to the modern-day Dipavali as suggested by some scholars, but it can also be the night of orgy in honour of the *yakshas*. *Kaumudi Jagat* was a folk festival which used to be celebrated on the night of *Ashvin Purnima*, the full-moon night of *Ashvin* month and encompassed lots of fun and frolic. *Suvasantaka* is nothing but *Madanotsava* held in honour of Madana or Kamadeva, the god of love. Holi, the boisterous festival of colours, is a relic of ancient *Madanotsava*.

All these festivals were celebrated with dance, music and drama performances wherein men and women participated in gay abandon. In Harsha's play, *Ratnavali*, there is a graphic description of this festival. According to *Kuttanimatam*, the beautiful *ganikas* of Varanasi, well versed in dance and music, used to perform the role of Ratnavali, describing the *Madanotsava*, when women would worship Kama and Rati.

The festivals help to infuse a romantic mood — the mood to flirt, to make love. In a number of love stories, young men and women on seeing each other for the first time fall in love during a festival. *Madanotsava* is most noted for the purpose.

A social gathering, *goshti* is yet another kind of diversion. It used to be held in the house of a rich citizen or of a beautiful *ganika*. Men and women gathered to discuss the arts and literature and to enliven the symposium, drink various kinds of wine and liquors like *madhu, maireya, sura* and *asava.*

Vatsyayana talks of drink parties, *samapanaka,* for men and women. Wine is considered as excellent stimulant to provoke the mood to love.

There are several intoxicant drinking scenes, *madhupana* in ancient and medieval sculptures and paintings. At the National Museum in New Delhi, a lovely piece of sculpture shows a drunk woman, most probably a *ganika,* being helped by her lover to stand on her feet. Gohil, in his *Grihyasutra,* refers to the custom of drenching the limbs of a young bride with wine. In the *chakrapuja* performed by *tantrics* before *maithuna,* men and women perform the ritual of drinking wine.

A picnic is considered a means of elevating one's mood. For the sake of fun, courtesans were invited to join in excursions and wine flew freely. Preferable locations were gardens, seashores and river-banks. In literature, there are several instances of picnics turning into bacchanal orgies.

Dance, drama and music were considered stimulants of sexual desire as also were aphrodisiacs of some kind. In the mansions of *ganika*s of ancient times, all these facilities were provided. In Shudraka's play, *Mricchakatika,* there is an elaborate description of a grand mansion of courtesan Vasantasena reverberating with dance, drama and music and with aroma of sensuous food. Readings of erotic plays were held. Vasantasena herself is shown to be a trained actress and dancer, adept in voice modulations—*Rangapraveshena kalanam chopashishaya, swaranaipunyamashrita.* Her mansion was like a complete entertainment industry in itself.

Shudraka says that while attending such dramatic entertainments, the man would sit by the side of his lady-love and flirt with her. When people became fully engrossed in witnessing the play, he would quietly slip away with her and take her to a convenient corner to make love.

Vatsyayana has given several tips to young men on how to seduce a girl. Those days a procuress was used to reach the girl. Jain or Buddhist nuns and female ascetics were favoured for the job as they had easy access to women in harems. In the play, *Malati Madhava* by Bhavabhuti, we find Buddhist nuns playing a major role in uniting the hero and the heroine. In Kalidasa's *Malvikagnimitra*, a similar role is played by a *parivrajika*, whom the jester straight away describes as a procuress, *pithamardika*. A common friend, *sakhi*, also plays a useful role. In the *Gita Govinda* of Jayadeva, it is a *sakhi* who helps to unite Radha with Krishna.

But there are also instances when sexually aroused male lovers, without waiting for their beloveds to appear, make love to the female intermediaries themselves.

Ancients have made clear demarcation between love and lust. In Shudraka's *Mricchakatika*, the heroine Vasantasena, a young and beautiful courtesan, says that a woman is attracted towards a young man due to his qualities: "You cannot make a girl fall in love by force — *gunah khalvanuragasya karanam, na punarbalatkarah*." Vatsyayana too considers mutual love as a reasonable incentive for marriage. Hence, of all the forms of marriage, he thinks the *gandharva* form is best because it is based on love, *anuraga*. At yet another place, he describes several types of sexual relationships but concludes that the best among them all is love-making based on intense love for each other, *ragavata rata*. He abhors casual relationships or a relationship forced upon the partner, or a relationship based on blind lust.

The best literary example of intense love, *anuraga*, is Rama's sorrow at Sita's abduction by Ravana, as narrated in the epic *Ramayana* by Valmiki. Vaishnavas thus differentiate between lust, *kama* and true love, *prema*. *Prema* is a sublime and spiritual love as exhibited by the divine couple, Radha and Krishna.

The *Taittiriya Upanishad* says that bliss, *ananda* is central to human existence. *Ananda* is Brahma. All are born of *ananda*; *ananda* sustains them. Ultimately, they merge into *ananda* as *ananda* is everything.

According to *Brihadaranyaka Upanishad*, the *upastha* or the procreative organ is the one and only source of *ananda* — *sarveshamanandanampuastha ekayanam*.

Sex is a basic instinct, *pravritti.* Hence, *Brihadaranyaka Upanishad* says that the human being is composed of desires — *kamamaya evayam purushah. Kama* is the essence of mind. *Brihadaranyaka Upanishad* further adds:

> Uddyalaka, son of Aruna, Nakamaudgalya and Kumarharit *rishi* have said that there are a number of ignorant Brahmins who perform the sexual act without knowing the science of it and this is certainly sinful.

Hence, Vatsyayana and his several predecessors as well as successors devised several techniques of enjoying sex in a correct manner. Defining *kama,* Vatsyayana says that all the five sense organs and their respective faculties are involved in the sexual act. *Kama* is a bliss which the mind experiences through all the five sense organs.

Hence, the various kinds of kisses and embraces, suggested by the authors of *Kamashastras,* aim at arousing and satisfying the sense organs. In addition, Vatsyayana and others speak of nail-marks and teeth-marks to be inflicted on the woman's body to arouse her sexually. Various erogenous zones of the body are marked for arousal through use of nails and teeth; different geometrical patterns are delicately and artistically marked on the body with nails and teeth. The nail-marks can be in the shape of half-moons, circles, lines, tigers' nails or claws, peacocks' feet, jumps of hares, leaves of blue lotuses. These marks can be made anywhere on the body but the most erogenous areas are supposed to be the armpit, the throat, the breasts, the lips, the *janghana* or the middle part of the body and the thighs. Different kinds of teeth marks include a faint bite, the swollen bite, the point, the line of points, the coral, the jewels, the broken clouds and the biting of the boar.

Vatsyayana has described sexual preferences, habits and practices of various countries. Different types of women too are described on the basis of their physical endowments and dispositions. Man is required to consider these factors before approaching a woman for sexual pleasure. Vatsyayana and others have also described the various kinds of congress and postures to be used during intercourse by way of variety and deriving utmost pleasure out of the sexual act.

It is said in the *Shastras* that man should observe keenly the sexual acts of different birds, animals and constantly devise new postures or *asanas* to enjoy his woman. While describing the different positions for coitus, a special, independent chapter is devoted to *purushayita* or woman on-top-of-the-man position.

About Kali, the *Yogini Tantra* says that she is constantly in congress with Shiva in the inverted position; she is called *viparitaratasakta*. The best illustration of this titillating posture is found sculpted in the Lakshmana temple at Khajuraho.

In the *Gita Govinda,* poet Jayadeva has described the *purushayita* practiced by Radha while sexually enjoying Krishna on the bank of River Yamuna. Of Radha, the poet, Jayadeva, says:

> Displaying her passion in the love-play,
> as the battle began,
> she launched a bold offensive.
> Above him,
> and triumphed over her lover.
> Her lips were still,
> her vine-like arm was slack,
> her chest was heaving,
> her eyes were closed.
> Why does a mood of manly force
> succeed for a woman in love? (Millar)

Of the various techniques employed for stimulation and intercourse, Vatsyayana describes in detail oral congress, *auparishtaka*. Fellatio is more common in Indian sculptural art and paintings and can be seen since second century BC. Cunnilingus is less frequent. Mutual oral congress scenes too are seen in temple art. However, Vatsyayana does not favour it.

Vatsyayana speaks of *apadravya* or the artificial male organ as a means of sexual gratification for woman. He briefly refers to homosexuality, *adhorata*. Group sex too is described. Groups in orgies are found in sculptural art since ancient times though some scholars consider them to be of ritualistic nature.

Orgies of all kinds, between one man and two women, one man many women, many men and one woman, a number of couples together and so on in sexual permutations and combinations are found sculpted on the temples of central India in particular. Temples in other regions too are found embellished with group orgies of this or that kind.

Bestiality involving men and women with animals in different postures and combinations is found portrayed in the Khajuraho group of temples, at Shishireshvara and Lingaraj temples at Bhubaneswar and at the Sun temple in Konark. However, this is not mentioned in literature.

Vatsyayana's *Kamasutra* has had a profound influence on Indian art, literature and society. In a story in *Panchatantra* by Pandit Vishnusharma, the friend of a young man who plans to meet the girl he loves, advises him to enjoy her according to the procedures of love-making, *vatsyayanotkta vidhi* — laid down by Vatsyayana. The great poet, Kalidasa, seems to be profoundly influenced by the *Kamasutra*. His descriptions of love scenes in *Kumarasambhava*, *Ritu Samhara*, *Meghadoota*, *Raghuvamsha* and plays like *Shakuntala*, *Vikramorvashiya* and *Malavikagnimitra* betray the influence of *Kamasutra*.

In Sri Harsha's, *Naishadhiyacharita,* there is an elaborate description of the honeymoon days spent by Nala and Damayanti and which not only makes frequent references to *Kamasutra* under different names, such as *Pushpashara-Shastra*, but even describes the romance between the hero and the heroine.

Bhavabhuti mentions the *Kamasutra* in the prologue of his play *Malati Madhava* and makes use of it whenever necessary.

A number of literary works, such as *Chaurapanchasika*, *Amaru Shataka*, *Sringarshataka* and the *Gita Govinda* do not hesitate to take recourse to the *Kamasutra*.

We can find visual representations of *Kamasutra* in sculptural art at Konark, Khajuraho, Bhubaneswar, Puri and other medieval temple sites, where plenty of similarity could be due to the fact that *Kamasutra* as also *belles-lettres*, sculpture and painting drew from the same cultural and social source.

Sringara or love is considered to be of two types — *vipralambha sringara* and *sambhoga sringara*. *Vipralambha sringara* means love in separation; it is a sentiment of love that is felt by the *nayak* and the *nayika* when they are not together. *Sambhoga sringara*, on the contrary, is the sentiment of love that turns erotic, mostly culminating in flirting or actual love-making between the man in love, *nayak* and the woman in love, *nayika* when they are together. It is love in union. When we say 'love in action' we mean 'love in union'. Descriptions of such love are not wanting in ancient literature.

In the larger and exalted context of the procreation of human race, there is a reference to cohabitation in the *Atharva Veda*. The hymn (14.2.66) says:

> O Bride, climb on this bed in a happy state of mind and create progeny for your husband. And like Indrani, get up before sunrise, in the early hours of the day.
>
> Even before, wise men have come to their wives and become close to them by properly cohabiting their bodies with those of their wives.
>
> O God, inspire a woman in whom I am going to sow my seed. Let her desire me and spread her legs for me and let me strike her procreative organ, *yoni*, with my *linga*, penis.
>
> O Bride, through your husband I clear the *yoni-marga* between your legs and I free you from the binding of Varuna created by Savita.
>
> O Man, ride over her loins, support her with your hands, with a happy mind bring her close to you, and create progeny.

The *Chandogya Upanishad* (II. XIII.1 and 2) has described the entire process of falling in love with a woman to cohabit with her in a beautiful verse. It speaks of approaching the woman with desire, courting and seducing her when fascinated by her, sleeping with her, passing time in love-making and deriving fulfilment.

However, all this was to explain the Vamadevya interwoven with the couple. But these passages in the *Vedas* and *Upanishads* are not there to titillate but are there as a part of spiritual musings.

Sringar is found in ample measure in the epics but seldom do we find overtly erotic passages or *sambhoga sringara* in them. In the story of Indra, the king of gods, and Ahalya, the beautiful wife of Sage Gautama, there is just a passing reference to *sambhoga sringara*. The epic *Ramayana,* which contains this story, says that both Indra and Ahalya enjoyed each other sexually and were gratified.

In *Gatha Saptashati,* there are a number of verses describing love in action. Some of them are quoted below:

> (*While making love*) just for a moment you acted like a man (*purushayite*), your hair got dishevelled, thighs started trembling, eyes dropped and fatigue set in; O beautiful one, rest for a moment and think how much man has to exert (in the act of love-making).
>
> He prides himself on being an expert in the act of love-making. She just tolerates (his atrocities) but thinking that she is relishing the act, the foolish lover enjoys her in a cruel way. Her body crumples like a delicate flower of *sirisha*.
>
> Just for a moment I saw her naked and was amazed (by her beauty). I thought I have found the treasure (of immense bliss), got the kingdom of heaven and drank deep from the elixir of life.
>
> Who is the most enjoyable woman sexually? A six-month pregnant one or one who has just returned from the stage by giving a dance performance or one who has delivered a baby one month ago: Son, make love to such a woman.
>
> The lover lifted up the face of his angry beloved, turned it towards him and made her drink wine from his mouth. She swallowed it as a panacea for her anger.
>
> An act of love-making, if performed out of mutual love, may it be at any place, done in any way, gives the lover immense pleasure. It surpasses the love-making performed according to the tenets of *Kamashastra*.
>
> Hail the embrace of a lover which is like a prologue to the drama of love-making (*ratinataka*). It gives pleasure to all the limbs. Just as in a gust of strong wind a tree gets uprooted, the resistance gets swept away by the sensuous embrace.
>
> After making love, the young bride could not find her clothes (to cover her). Hence, the bashful one embraced her lover so that he could not see her middle part any more.

> After intense love-making, the woman closed her eyes out of the pleasure she received. However, her rustic lover thought her to be dead and ran away in fright.

Kalidasa, the great Indian poet, is considered a master of *sringara rasa* or lyrical sentiment of love and eroticism. We find fine depictions of both *vipralambha* and *sambhoga sringaras* in his poetic works. At many places, he is highly erotic and frankly describes love in action.

The sexual life of King Agnivarna has been described by Kalidasa with great relish. He says:

> As the king was fond of a new companion, every time due to the fear that they may be discarded too, women used to leave him in the middle of love-making, unsatiated, so that his interest in them may not wane and they may be called again and again to fulfil his carnal desires and passion.
>
> When, during love-making, he tried to kiss the lips of the women, they would turn away their faces and while he tried to unknot their lower garments, they would resist the move; they would not allow him to do anything he wanted to do and thus increase his sexual passion through coquetry.
>
> When women used to get tired after prolonged love-making, they used to rub their lovely breasts, smear with the cool paste of sandalwood on the chest of the king and sleep above him as if they were practicing the *Kamasutra* posture, in which the woman lies on the chest of her lover, slowly hitting him with her breasts and finally hold him in a tight embrace.
>
> In the summer months, women used to smear their lovely breasts with the cool paste of sandalwood, wear pearl jewellery and suspend the girdle with gems over their hips so that they would satisfy the king with their passionate love-making. At that time, the king used to drink wine by placing the mango blossom and the flower of *patala* in it to arouse his passion, which got dimmed after the passing of *Vasanta ritu.*

The love-life of King Agnivarna was very rich. He was so handsome that women used to throw themselves at him. He was fond of making love in the bowers on the bed made of delicate flowers. Apprehensive of his secret trysts with lovely women getting reported to his queens by the palace-maids, he used to placate them by making love to them. He swam with beautiful women in ponds, taught them different kinds of acting and made them perform; with them, he would visit the drinking dens; escape from the palace to make love to other women; take them to sit on the swing. Kalidasa has portrayed all this in his poem.

In his lyrical poem, *Meghadoota*, Kalidasa has described the love-life of *yakshas* of Alakapuri and who were fond of drinking wine on the terraces of their mansions to arouse their passion. Their women were very beautiful. When lovers untying the knot of their lower garments, tried to remove their clothes with the intention of making love to them, out of shyness they would throw *gulal* powder on the lamps of lustrous gems which emitted light, to extinguish them. They would forget that gem-lamps could not be put off by such measures as they were not ordinary oil-lamps. However, basically, this poem is about love in separation, *vipralambha sringar.*

In his lovely poem *Ritusamhara*, Kalidasa has described the natural beauty of six seasons of the year — *Grishma*, *Varsha*, *Sharada*, *Hemanta*, *Shishira* and *Vasanta* — and the love-life of people during these respective seasons.

However, in his epic, *Kumarasambhava*, Kalidasa turns frankly erotic while describing the love tryst of Shiva with his beautiful newly-married bride, Parvati. Kalidasa beautifully describes how a shy bride opposes her husband's advances to remove her clothes, and on being made naked, shuts his eyes with her hands, becoming quite adept in the art of love-making.

Chourapanchashika by Bilhana Kavi is a unique lyrical poem with fifty verses composed in the eleventh century. Thus, its central theme is a poet who has a secret love affair with the beautiful daughter of his patron king. When the king comes to know about this, he orders his execution. On the way to the gallows, he remembers his lovely beloved and his intense love-making to her. His poetic utterances are described as purely erotic giving minute and often charming details of the past scenes of happy love. He remembers her actions, emotions, movements before, during and after love-making in a brazenly erotic manner. Here are a few stanzas from the work describing the love in action, *sambhoga sringara:*

> To this day, I remember her who (being very delicate) was unable to tolerate the travails of love-making, whose curly, black, dishevelled hair spread on her fair cheeks, though trembling with the idea of sin she was committing secretly, did encircle my neck with her lovely hands.
>
> To this day I remember her whose limbs had become shaky due to drinking, who was slim but bent by the weight of her heavy hips and breasts, whose face was like a full moon, whose dishevelled hair came cascading on it and which acted as a string holder of the wild dance of love-making — *surata-tandava-sutradhari.*
>
> In this very moment, even in next birth I will remember that beloved of mine whose eyes, dancing with joy during the course of love-making, automatically got closed (to savour the bliss of pleasurable intercourse) at the end of it, whose body became relaxed and languid, hair dishevelled and clothes in disarray falling away from her lovely body. She was looking like a beautiful swan swiftly gliding in the forest of lotus flowers of amour.
>
> To this day I remember her cheeks, which were hit by golden ear-rings during the course of *viparitarati-krida* (woman on top-of- the-man sexual posture) and the face which was adorned with large, pearl-like, drops of perspiration caused by exertion due to circular motion of the body.
>
> To this day I remember her passionate glances before love-making, her shattered limbs during intercourse, nail-marks on her beautiful breasts when her clothes fell apart and teeth marks on her red lips.
>
> To this day I remember the not-too-distinct, sweet words uttered by my beloved, whose meaning was not clear and which were uttered in a trembling voice due to the fatigue caused by rigorous love-making. But still they sounded very enchanting to my ears.
>
> I still remember the nail-marks made by me on her golden thighs during the act of love-making and which I noticed when I pulled her clothes again (with the intention of making love once again) and her moving away with shyness to cover those marks with her delicate hands.

Equally erotic is the twelfth-century poet Jayadeva's lyrical composition, the *Gita Govinda*. He calls it *srivasudeva-ratikeli-katha* or the story of amorous sports of Sri and Vasudeva or that of Radha and Krishna. He invites readers who are interested in *vilas-kala* or the art of love-making to read his poem. We find several verses describing both *vipralambha* and *sambhoga sringaras*.

Jayadeva is quite open in describing love in union. His Radha remembers the twinkling of her jewelled anklets and ringing of bells attached to her girdle when Krishna makes love to her and kisses her in the end, after his amour has been satiated. She remembers languor set in her limbs and closes her lotus eyes due to blissful intercourse with her lover, *rati-sukhas*.

A friend advises Radha, with heavy hips, to rush to the forest on the bank of River Yamuna for blissful love-making, or *rati-sukha*, where Vanamali Krishna, whose hands playfully rub the beautiful breasts of cowherd girls, is waiting for her. She asks her to remove the girdle, discard the clothes and 'unite your *janghana* with his in *viparita rati* posture'.

In the seventh *sarga*, we see Radha imagining Krishna making love to a beautiful cowherd girl. She describes her as *rati-ranadhira* or expert in the war, that is, love-making and one who sighs with pleasure, *bahuvidhakujitaratirasarasita*, during love-making.

In the concluding *sarga*, there is a very erotic and frank description of love-making between Radha and Krishna, including *viparitarati* performed by Radha.

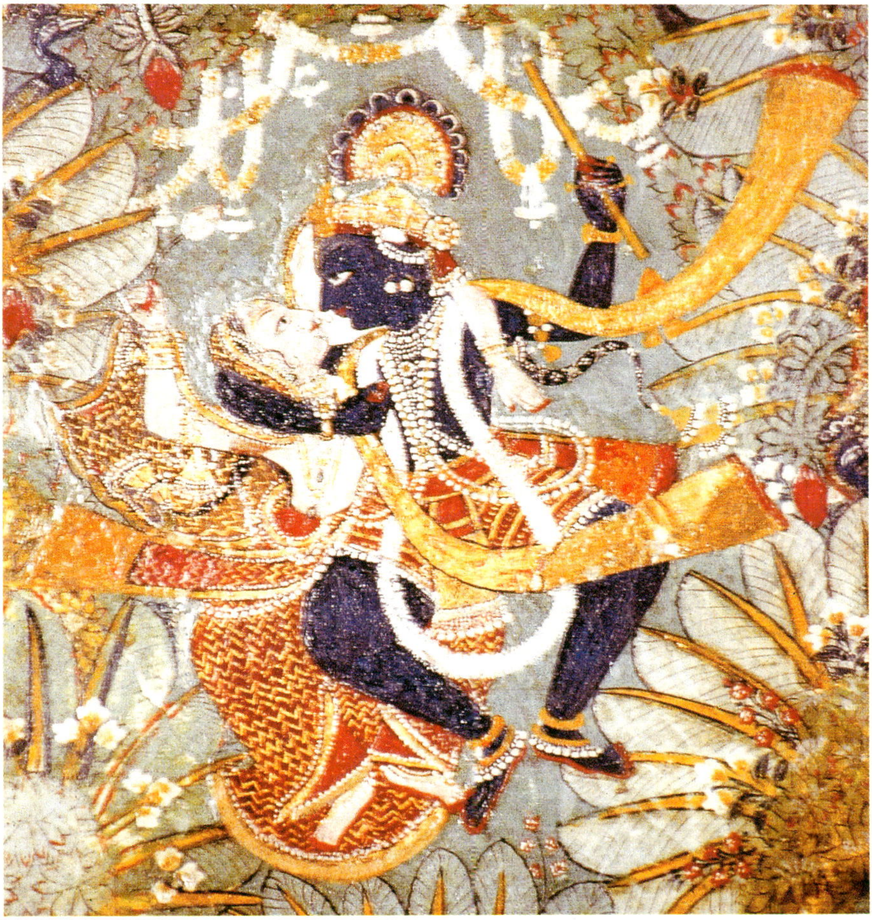

Krishna dancing with Radha in gay abandon

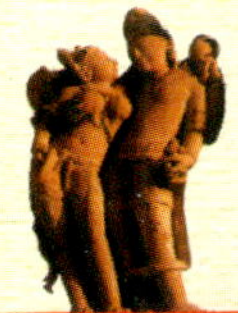

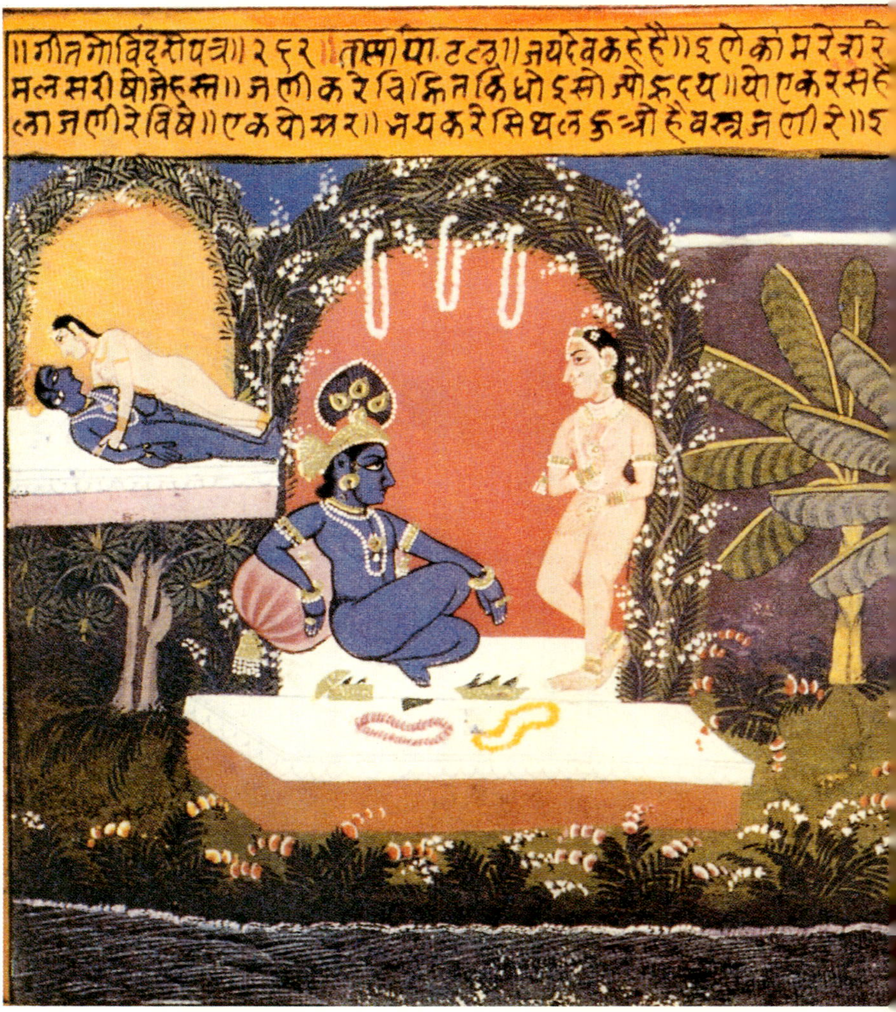

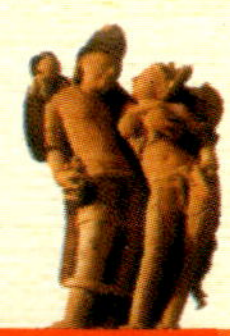

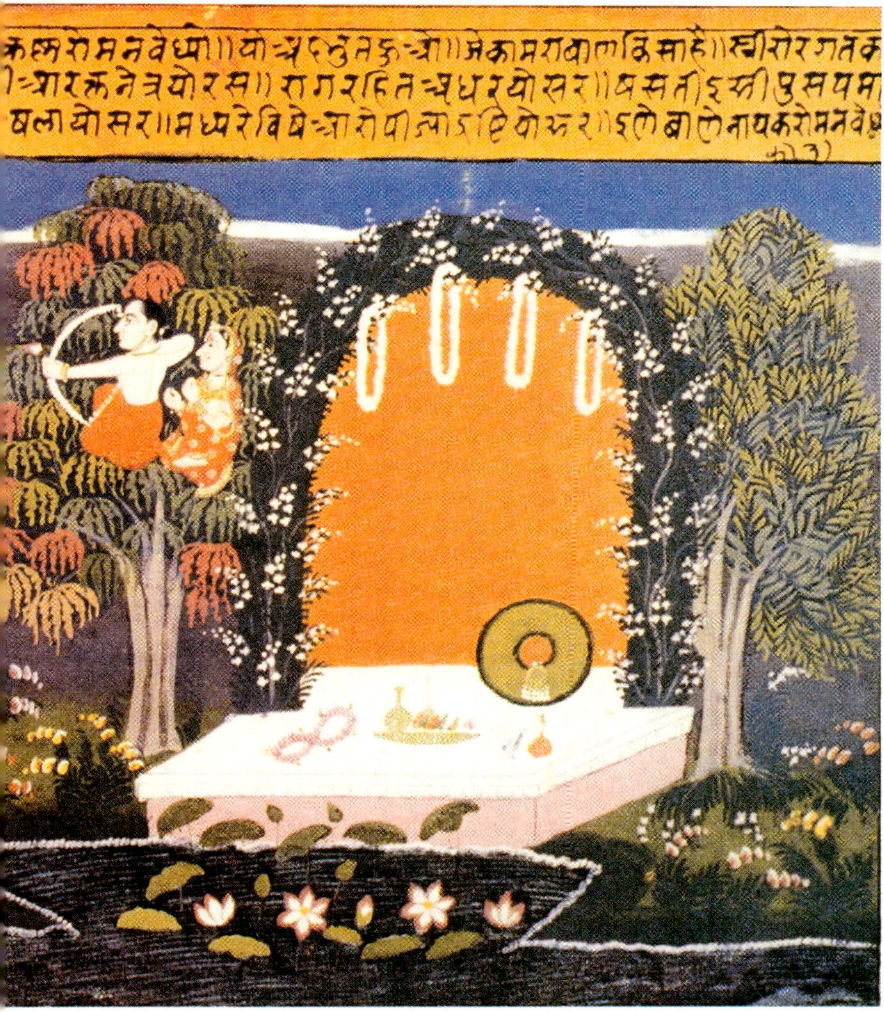

Krishna and Radha struck by Kama's arrow of love

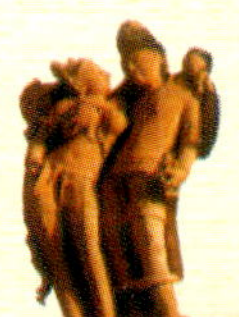

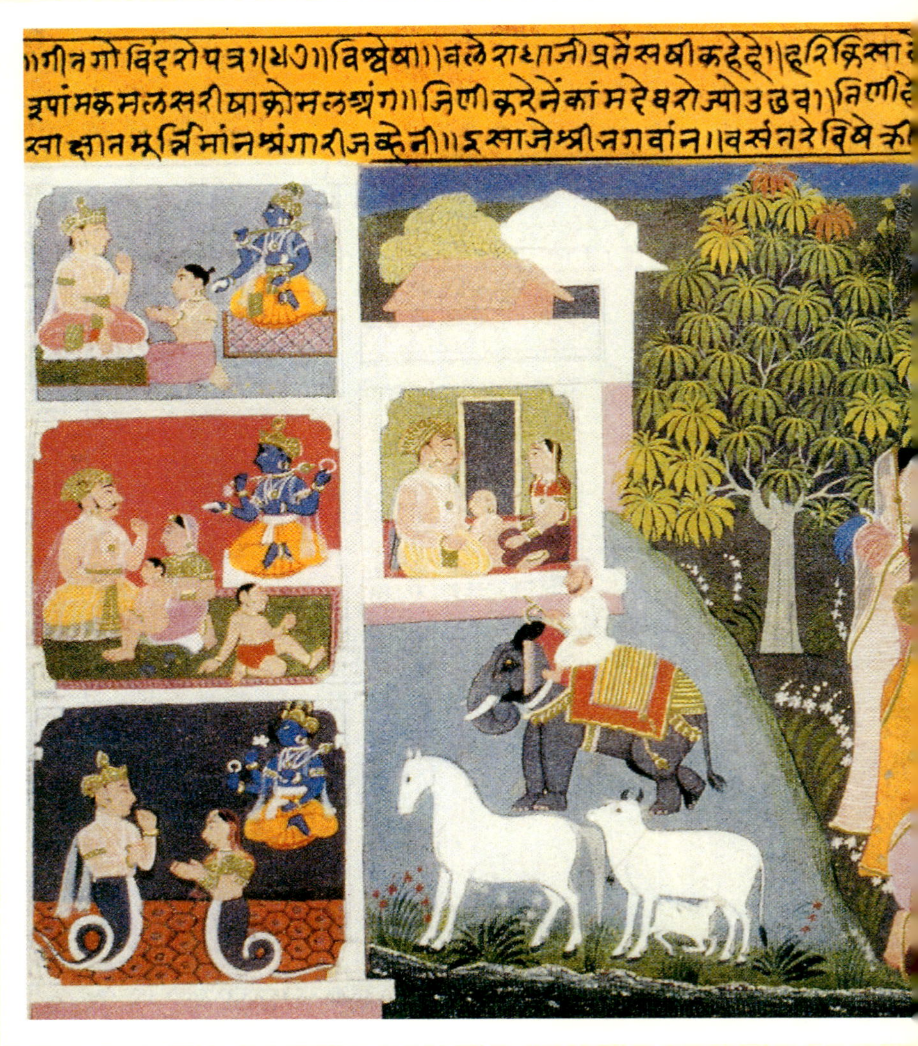

Krishna showering love on gopis to bring joy and bliss (ananda). *In the left-hand corner, Krishna is seen bestowing his blessings on kings*

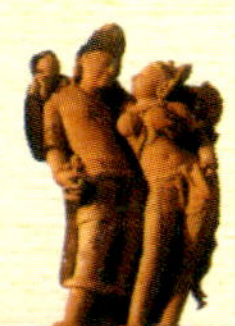

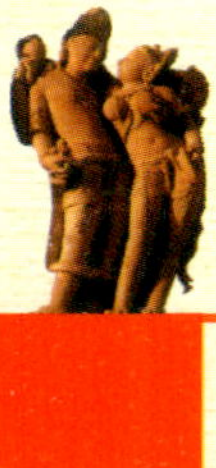

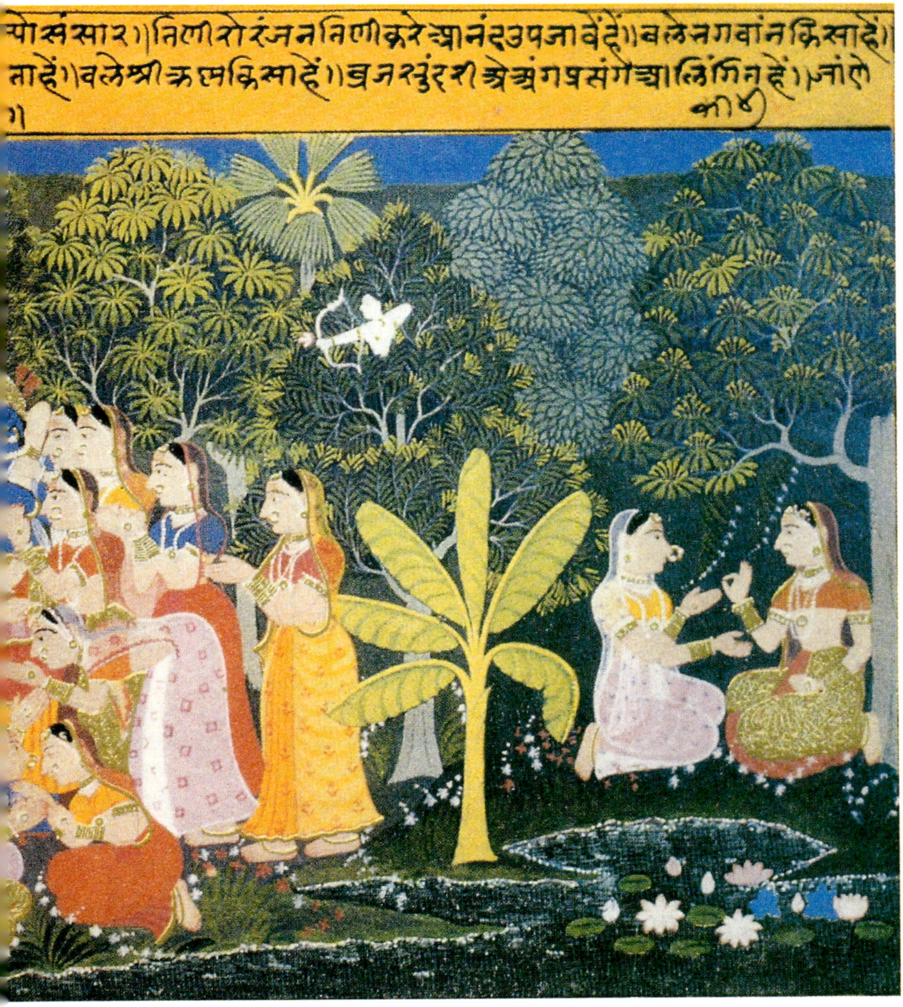

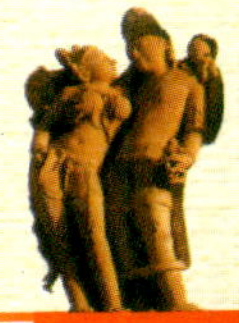

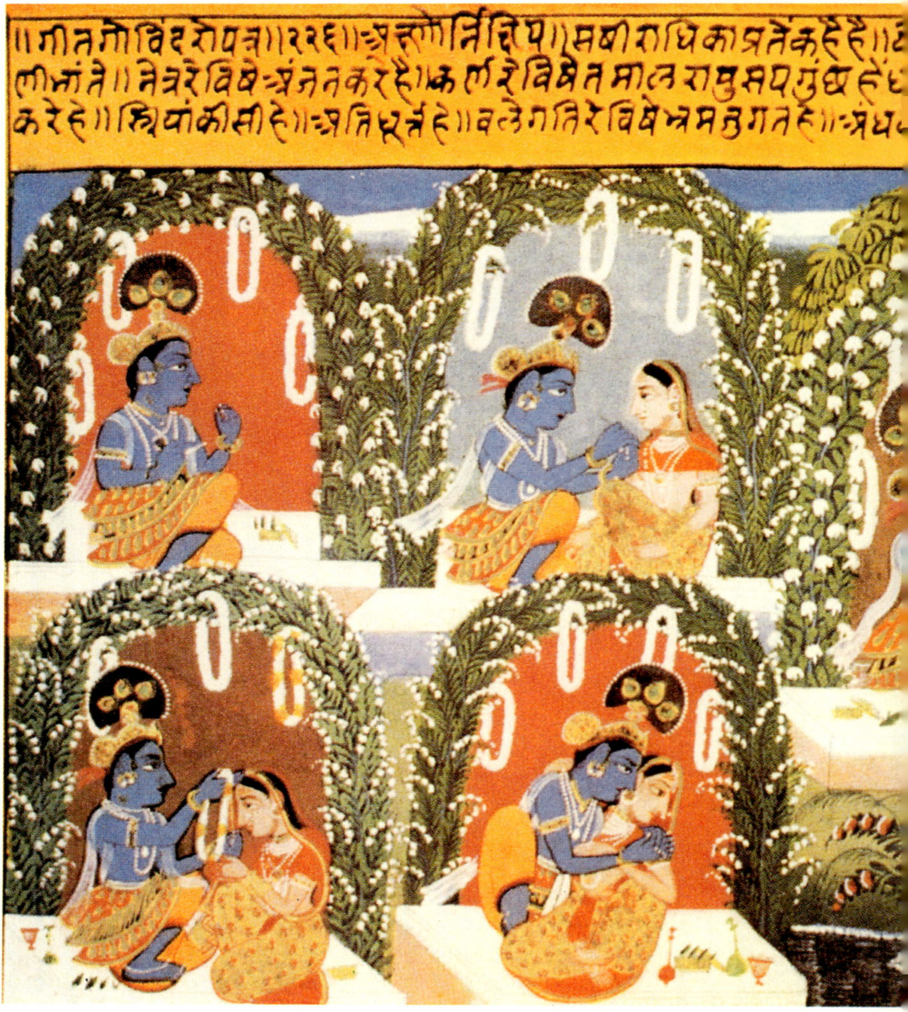

Krishna embracing Radha after wooing her in different ways

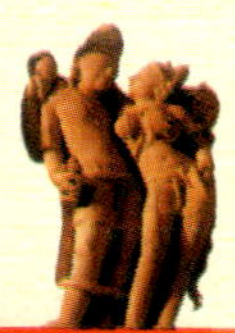

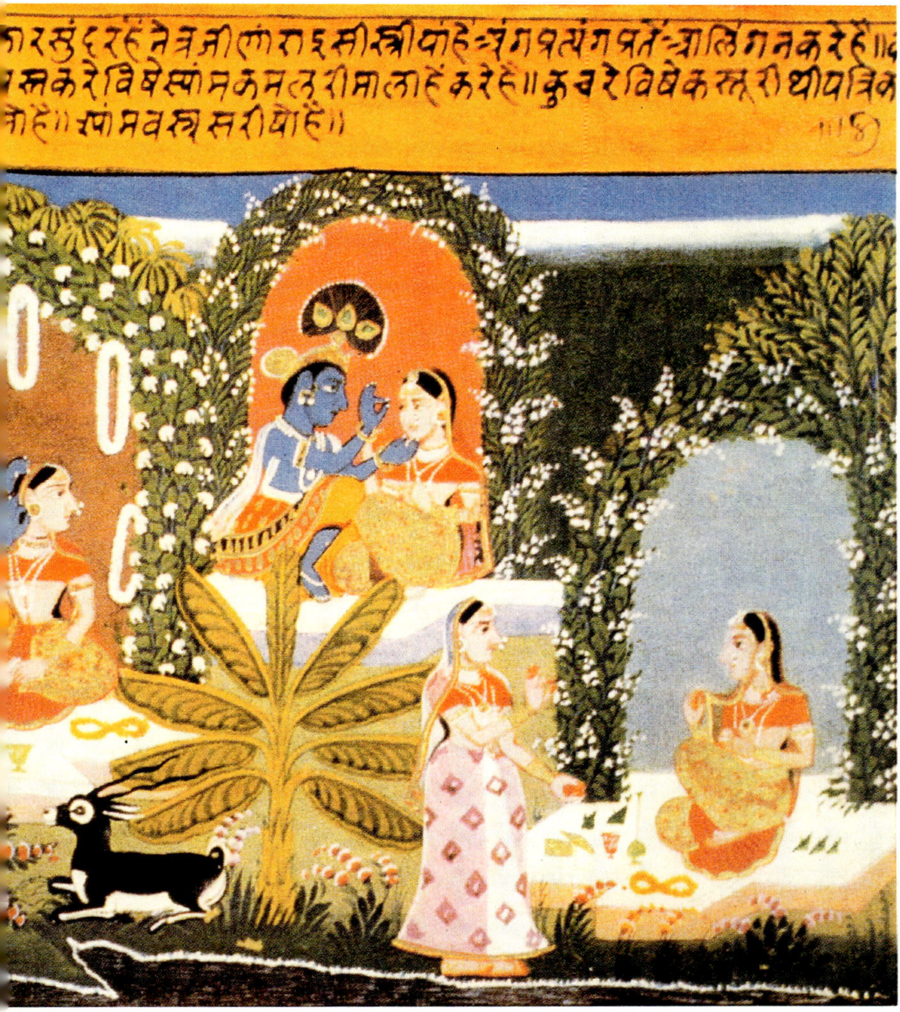

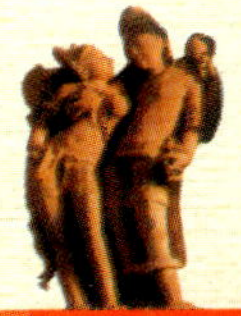

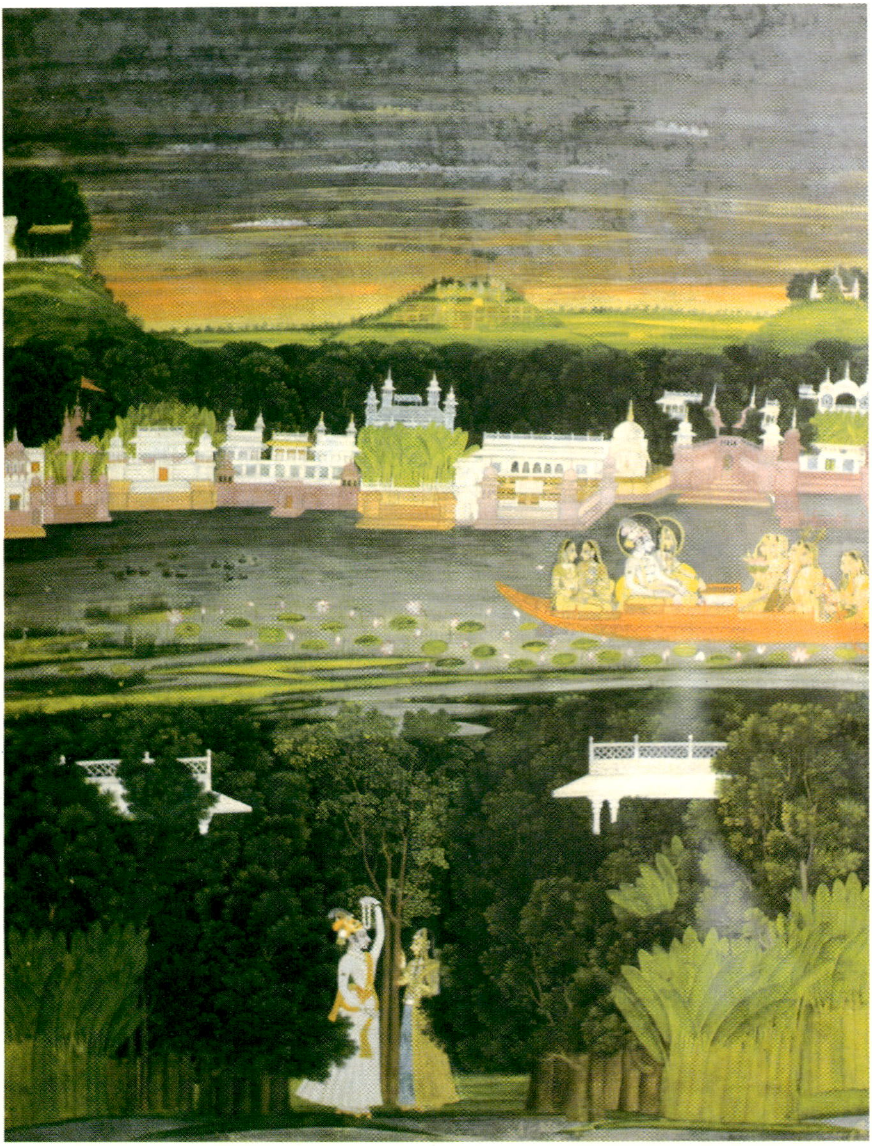

Radha and Krishna in the boat of love

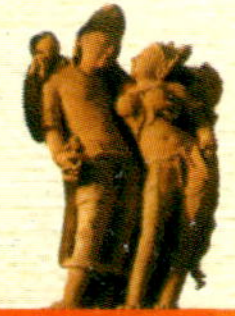

Chapter Nine

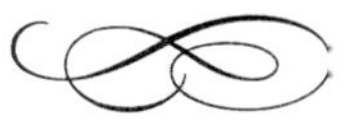

CULT OF LOVE

A cult is a system of religious beliefs with excessive admiration for a person or a concept. When an idea of love between a divine pair becomes the focal point of a religious system, we call it the cult of love. In Vrindavan, on the bank of river Yamuna where love between dark-hued Krishna and beautiful cowherd girls, fair as *champak* flowers, becomes the centre of a religious system, we tend to call it a cult of love.

Love between Radha and Krishna became the theme of one of the beautiful verses, *Gatha,* in Maharashtri Prakrit in the first century AD. But Radha of the *Gatha* was then not a worshipped divinity. She was just a playful companion of Krishna belonging to the cowherd community. By third century AD, when *Devi Bhagavata* was written, Radha acquired an individual status. She came to be described as primordial energy, *mula-prakriti* and the presiding deity of *shaktipitha* of Vrindavan. In the fifth century AD, the story entitled *Panchatantra* Radha is referred to as Lakshmi.

At Paharpur in Rajashahi district of Bengal, a great dwelling place, *vihara* of a Pala ruler, Dharmapala, was excavated and it was constructed with bricks. Percy Brown writes:

> For the instruction and edification of the multitudes of devotees who paid homage to this shrine, as it is recorded that it was venerated by the followers of all creeds, Buddhist, Hindu and Jain, the exterior

> faces of the terraces were embellished with a continuous series of terracotta plaques illustrated in bas relief, depicting the mythology and folklore of the country. Among the subjects depicted, incidents have been identified related to the life of God Krishna, said to be antedate to the emergence of this cult by several centuries.

The excavated structure is ascribed to eighth century AD. It is at Paharpur that the first image of Radha-Krishna together was found.

Despite the tremendous popularity of the cult of love in Bengal, it was only since the seventeenth century that a few Radha-Krishna temples were built there. There are a few in Braj region too and the only temple of significance dedicated to Radha is located at Barasana. However, Radha-Krishna love is the most popular theme in various schools of Indian miniature paintings.

Though it is a fact that it was after Jayadeva wrote his immortal poem *Gita Govinda* that the cult of the Radha-Krishna love attained a high stature; it was not that during the intervening period of Maharashtrian Prakrit that poets of the first century AD sang of their love and Jayadeva wrote his poem in the twelfth century, nobody wrote about Radha-Krishna. A number of Sanskrit and Prakrit poets have referred to them. Even in three inscriptions of Vakpati Munja, the tenth-century Parmar ruler of Malva, there is a reference to Krishna suffering the pangs of separation from Radha. The eleventh-century treatise on dramaturgy, *Natya Darpana*, by Ramachandra Gunachandra refers to the play *Radhika Vipralambha* by poet Bejjala, who is ascribed to tenth century AD.

However, no writer of poetry and drama acknowledged the divine stature of Radha in relation to Krishna till Jayadeva elevated her to the stature of a cult figure.

Jayadeva, in the very first poem of the first canto of his *Gita Govinda,* calls Radha as Sri, the goddess of beauty, success and wealth, and describes his poem as the story of the amorous sports of Sri, that is Radha, and Vasudeva, that is Krishna. In the text also, he refers to her by her divine names such as Padmavati, Kamala, Lakshmi and Chandi. There is a temple of Goddess Kamala in the premises of Jagannatha temple where he used to sing his poem.

Lord Jagannatha is identified with Krishna. We do not know if Goddess Kamala, in the premises of this temple, was in Jayadeva's mind when he addressed Radha as Kamala.

The focus of the poem is on *rati-keli*, the amorous sport of love-making. He invites the audience who are interested to learn more about the *vilas kala* to read his poem. As a form of literature, he has described Radha as the *nayika* in eight different modes, as described by Bharata in his *Natya Shastra*.

Jayadeva founded the cult of love involving two divinities. In this extremely erotic poem, the main theme is love in different modes while the characters involved in love are somewhat secondary. Love became supreme in this cult. Savouring of the love between Radha and Krishna became the main theme.

Gita Govinda achieved the status of a sacred hymn and the tradition of reciting it in temples came into vogue. Prataparudradeva, the Gajapati ruler of Orissa, in his Oriya inscription of July 1499 on the western front of the Jagannatha temple, ordained that the *Gita Govinda* should be sung and performed every day in the *Nata Mandir* of Jagannatha temple. This tradition reached the distant land of Kerala too. The *Gita Govinda* came to be sung in a number of temples as a part of ritual service. Inscription of Sarangadeva's reign, dated to 1290, opens with the stanza of '*Dashavatara Ashtapadi*' from the *Gita Govinda*.

After Jayadeva, several poets wrote profusely, extolling the cult of love of Radha-Krishna practically in all parts of the country. Chandidas in Bengal and Vidyapati in Mithila topped the list. The cult threw up new apostles and prophets of the cult and with them, came into vogue new concepts and ideas of love, expanding the horizon of the cult.

The most significant among them was Chaitanya Mahaprabhu about whom his followers said that he was no less than Radha and Krishna incarnated in a single body. He intensely longed for Krishna, just as a desperate Radha in the event of a separation would have done and this condition came to be described as *Radhabhava* or *mahabhava*.

A.K. Ramanujan in his article 'On Women Saints' in the book,

Divine Consort, has made a very interesting observation on the cult of devotion, *bhakti.* He has said:

> An especially arresting aspect of the *bhakti* milieu, however, is the extent to which *bhakti* itself appears as 'feminine' in nature by contrast to Vedic sacrifice, which may be considered 'masculine' in ethos, personnel and language. The chief mood of *bhakti* is the erotic (*sringara*), seen almost entirely from an Indian woman's point of view, whether in the phase of separation or of union. Thus, when saints, both male and female, address love poems to Krishna and Shiva and adopt such feminine personae as wife (*kanta*), illicit lover (*parakiya*), trystic woman (*abhisarika*), and even Radha herself, they are drawing on a long, rich history (p. 316).

Chaitanya was under the influence of *mahabhava* almost every moment of the day. His disciples have defined the contours of his cult of love as an extension of the one floated by Jayadeva, Chandidas, Vidyapati and others. They have said:

> Radha is in fact a blissful potency, *haldini shakti,* of Krishna who took incarnation on earth to spread *madhurya* or sweetness, the feelings of tender affection and love. *Sringara rasa,* the erotic sentiment, is the highest form or *madhurya* and that too in *parakiya bhava.*

Swakiya means 'your own' and *parakiya* means 'one belonging to the other'. It was believed that the intensity of love is more in the case of *parakiya* as it is fraught with danger. Radha was a *parakiya* with whom Krishna established an illicit love-relationship.

Dr Shashibhushan Dasgupta states in his *Obscure Religious Cults*:

> With the popularity of the Radha-Krishna songs, the ideal of *parakiya rati,* or unconventional love between man and woman not bound by conjugal ties became emphasised.

In almost all the theological discussions of the Vaishnavas of the post-Chaitanya period, the superiority of the ideal of love, *parakiya,* to that of *swakiya* was variously interpreted.

In his *Typical Selections from the Old Bengali Literature* (Vol. II, pp.1638-1643), Dr D.C. Sen has quoted from two old documents, belonging to the first half of the eighteenth century, where we find that regular debates were arranged between the Vaishnava exponents of the *parakiya* and *swakiya* ideals of love, and in the debates, the upholders of the *swakiya* view were sadly defeated and had to sign documents admitting the supremacy of the *parakiya* ideal of love. This will help us in gauging how great an influence this *parakiya* ideal exerted on the people of the time belonging to the Vaishnava fold. This ideal of love, *parakiya,* has been the strongest factor in moulding the doctrines of Sahajiya Vaishnavism of Bengal (p. 119).

In the Brindavan of sixteeenth century AD, a number of love cults with Radha and Krishna as their presiding icons emerged, throwing up new concepts. All these cults around the Radha-Krishna love came to be known as *rasika sampradaya*, evolving the idea of *nikunja lila* and *nitya vihar*.

According to this concept, in the beautiful woods and its bowers on the bank of River Yamuna, the amorous sport of love-making between Radha and Krishna continues to this day. *Jivatma,* in the form of a *sakhi* of the couple, watches this *krida* and derives spiritual pleasure from it.

Nimbark, Chaitanya and Pusti *sampradayas* of the Braj region have contributed to this concept but it was Hita Harivamsha of the Radha-Vallabha *sampradaya,* who took it to new heights. Hita Harivamsha wrote some beautiful poems describing the *nikunja lila* of Radha and Krishna, some of which are given below and which were translated by F.S. Growse.

> I. Whatever my Beloved doeth is pleasing to me; and whatever is pleasing to me, that my Beloved doeth. The place where I would be is in my Beloved's eyes; and my Beloved would fain be the apple of my eyes. My love is dearer to me than body, soul, or life; and my love would lose a thousand lives for me. (Rejoice Sri Hit Hari Vans!) The loving pair, one dark, one fair, is like two cygnets; tell me, who can separate wave from water?

> II. O my Beloved, has the fair spoken? This is surely a beautiful night; the lightning is folded in the lusty cloud's embrace. O friend, where is

the woman who would quarrel with so exquisite a prince of gallants? (Rejoice, Sri Hit Hari Vans!) Dear Radhika hearkened with her ears and with voluptuous emotion joined in love's delights.

III. At daybreak, the wanton pair, crowned with victory in love's conflict, were all-exuberant. On her face are frequent beads of labour's dew, and all the adornments of her person are in disarray, the paint-spot on her brow is all but effaced by heat, and the straggling curls upon her lotus face resemble roaming bees. (Rejoice, Sri Hit Hari Vans!) Her eyes are red with love's colours and her voice and loins feeble and relaxed.

IV. Your face, fair dame, today is full of joy, betokening your happiness and delight in the intercourse with your Beloved. Your voice is languid and tremulous, your pretty *tilak* half effaced, the flowers on your head faded, and the parting of your hair as if you had never made it at all. The Bountiful One of his grace refused you no boon, as you coyly took the hem of your robe between your teeth. Why shrink away so demurely? You have changed clothes with your Beloved, and the dark-hued swain has subdued you as completely as though he had been tutored by a hundred Loves. The garland on his breast is faded, the clasp of his waist-belt loose (Rejoice, Sri Hit Hari Vans!) as he comes from his couch in the bower.

V. Today at dawn there was a shower of rapture in the bower, where the happy pair was delighting themselves, one dark, one fair, bright with all gay colours, as she tripped with dainty foot upon the floor. Great Syam, the glorious lord of love, had his flower wreath stained with the saffron dye of her breasts, was embellished with the scratches of his darling's nails; she too was marked by the hands of her jewel of lovers. The happy pair in an ecstasy of affection make sweet song, stealing each other's heart (Rejoice, Sri Hit Hari Vans!). The bard is fain to praise, but the drone of a bee is as good as his ineffectual rhyme.

VI. Who so clever, pretty damsel, whom her lover comes to meet, stealing through the night? Why shrink so coyly at my words? Your eyes are suffused and red with love's excitement, your bosom is marked with his nails, you are dressed in his clothes, and your voice is tremulous. (Rejoice, Sri Hit Hari Vans!) Radha's amorous lord has been mad with love.

VII. Today the lusty swain and blooming dame are sporting in their pleasant bower. O list! Great and incomparable is the mutual affection of the happy pair, on the heavenly plain of Brindaban. The ground gleams bright with coral land crystal and there is a strong odour of camphor. A dainty couch of soft leaves is spread, on which the dark groom and his fair bride recline, intent upon the joys and delights of dalliance, their lotus cheeks stained with red streaks of betel juice. There is a charming struggle between dark hands and fair to loosen the string that binds her skirt. Beholding herself as in a mirror in the necklace on Hari's breast, the silly girl is troubled by delusion and begins to fret, till her lover wagging his pretty chin shows her that she has been looking only at her own shadow. Listening to her honeyed voice, as again and again she cries 'Nay, nay,' Lalita and the others take a furtive peep (Rejoice, Sri Hit Hari Vans!) till tossing her hands in affected passion, she snaps his jewelled necklet.

VIII. Ah, red indeed are your lotus eyes, lazily languishing and inflamed by night-long watch, and their collyrium all faded. From your drooping eyelids shoots a glance like a bolt that strikes your swain as it were a deer and he cannot stir. (Rejoice, Sri Hit Hari Vans!) O damsel, voluptuous in motion as the swan, your eyes deceive even the wasps and bees.

IX. Radha and Mohan are such a dainty pair: he dark and beautiful as the sapphire, she with body of golden lustre; Hari with a *tilak* on his broad forehead and the fair with a *roli* streak amidst the tresses of her hair; the lord like a stately elephant in gait and the daughter of Vrishabhanu like an elephant queen; the damsel in a blue vesture and Mohan in yellow with a red *khaur* on his forehead (Rejoice, Sri Hit Hari Vans!) Radha's amorous lord is dyed deep with love's colours.

X. Today the damsel and her swain take delight in novel ways. What can I say? They are altogether exquisite in every limb; sporting together with arms about each other's neck and cheek to cheek, by such delicious contact making a circle of wanton delight. As they dance, the dark swain and the fair damsel, pipe and drum and cymbal blend in sweet concert with the tinkling of the bangles on her wrists and ankles and the girdle round her waist. (Sri Hit Hari Vans!). Rejoicing at the sight of the damsels' dancing and their measured paces, tears his soul from his body and lays them both at their feet.

XI. The pavilion is a bright and charming spot; Radha and Hari are in glistening attire and the full-orbed autumnal moon is resplendent in the heaven. The dark-hued swain and nymph of golden sheen, as they toy together, show like the lightning's flash and sombre cloud. In saffron vestment he and she in scarlet, their affection deep beyond compare, and the air, cool, soft and laden with perfumes. Their couch is made of leaves and blossoms and he woos her in dulcet tones, while coyly the fair one repulses his every advance. Love tortures Mohan's soul, as he touches her bosom, or waist-band, or wreath, and timorously she cries 'off, off'. Pleasant is the sporting of the glorious lord, close-locked in oft-repeated embrace, and like an earth-reviving river is the flood of his passion.

XII. Come Radha, you knowing one, your paragon of lovers has started a dance on the bank of the Jamuna's stream. Bevies of damsels are dancing in all the abandonment of delight; the joyous pipe gives forth a stirring sound. Near the Bansi-bat, a sweetly pretty spot, where the spicy air breathes with delicious softness, where the half-opened jasmine fills the world with overpowering fragrance, beneath the clear radiance of the autumnal full moon, the milkmaids with raptured eyes are gazing on your glorious lord, all beautiful from head to foot, quick to remove love's every pain. Put your arms about his neck, fair dame, pride of the world, and lapped in the bosom of the ocean of delight, disport yourself with Syam in his blooming bower.

Thus, the cult of love is still in existence with a huge following of Vaishnava community, particularly of Braj and Bengal.

The Buddhist *Sahajiya* cult of Bengal in conjunction with Vaishnava love cult gave rise to the *Vaishnava Sahajiya* cult, a tantric branch of the cult of love.

In *Cultural Heritage of India*, Vol. IV, p 296, S.B. Dasgupta writes:

Sahaja or Absolute divides itself into two, as the lover and beloved, and enjoyer and enjoyed, as Krishna and Radha; this playful division of the one into two is for nothing but self-realisation. In terms of the *Sahajiyas*, the *sahaja* manifests itself into two currents: *rasa* (love) and *rati* (the exciting cause of love and the support of love), and these two currents of *rasa* and *rati* are represented by Krishna and Radha. Again it is held that man and woman on earth are but physical representations of Krishna and Radha, or *rasa* and *rati* of Gokola; in the corporeal forms, man and woman represent the *rupa,* external manifestation of Krishna and Radha, who reside, so to speak, in every man and woman as the true spiritual self, *swarupa*. The *sadhana* consists first in realisation of *swarupa* in *rupa*, and after this realisation the pair should unite in love; the realisation of infinite bliss that follows from such a union is the highest spiritual gain.

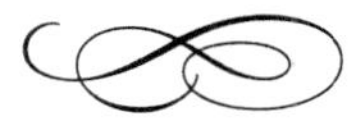

Select Bibliography

Agehananda, Bharati : *Tantric Tradition*, Anchor Books, Doubleday & Co., New York, 1970.

Anand, Mulk Raj : *Kama Sutra of Vatsyayana*, Arnold-Heinneman, 1990.

Agrawala, V. S. : *Bharatiya Kala*, Prithvi Prakashan, New Delhi, 1966.

Banerji, S.C. : *Society in Ancient India,* D.K. Printworld, 1993.

Basham, A.L.: *The Wonder that was India*, Rupa Co., New Delhi, 2002.

: *A Cultural History of India*, Oxford, 1980.

Coomaraswami, A.K.: *History of Indian and Indonesian Art*, Munshiram Manoharlal, New Delhi, 1972.

Damodaragupta: *Kuttanimatam*, Mira Prakashan, 1980.

Dasgupta, Shashibhusan: *Obscure Religious Cults*, Firma KLM, Calcutta, 1975.

De, Sushil Kumar: *Ancient Indian Erotics and Erotic Literature*, Firma KLM, Calcutta, 1959.

Desai, Devangana : *Erotic Sculpture of India*, Tata McGraw Hill, 1976.

Dhere, R.C. : *Lajjagauri*, Srividya Prakashan, Pune, 1988.

Dutta, Manmathanath : *Mahanirvan Tantra*, Chowkhamba, Varanasi, 1979.

Growse, F.S., Mathura, A : *A District Memoir*, Asian Educational Services, 1979.

Howley, J.S. : *The Divine Consort*, Harvard University, 1982.

Jayadeva : *Ratimanjiri*, Chowkhamba, Varanasi, 1988.

Kavishekhar Kalyan Malla : *Anangaranga*, Chowkhamba, Varanasi, 1987.

Kokkoka : *Ratirahasya*, Krishnadas Akademi, 1994.

Macdonell, A.A : *Vedic Mythology*, Motilal Banarasidas, New Delhi, 2002.

Meyer, J.J : *Sexual Life in Ancient India*, Motilal Banarasidas, New Delhi, 1989.

Millar, Barbara Stoler : *Love Song of Dark Lord* (Jayadeva's *Gita Govinda*), Columbia University Press, 1977.

Mittal, Prabhudayal: *Braj ke Dharmasampradayon ka Itihas* (Hindi), National Publishing House, New Delhi, 1963.

Mukherjee, R.: *The Culture and Art of India*, Allen & Unwin, 1959.

Nath, R.: *The Art of Khajuraho*, Abhinav Publications , New Delhi, 1980.

Padmashri: *Nagarasarvaswam*, Chowkhamba, Varanasi, 2002.

Pandit, R.S.: *River of Kings* (*Rajatarangini*), Sahitya Akademi, New Delhi, 1977.

Praudhadevarajamaharaj: *Ratiratnapradipika*, Krishnadas Akademi, 2002.

Rowland, Benjamin : *The Art and Architecture of India*, Penguin Books, Middlesex, 1967.

Sarma, Kedarnath : *Kathasaritsagara*, B.R. Parishad, 2000.

Sastri, Devadatta (ed.) : *The Kamasutra*, Chowkhamba, Varanasi, 1964.

Sastri, Nilakantha and Srinivasachari : *Advanced History of India*, Allied Publishers, New Delhi, 1970.

Sivapriyanand, Swami : *A South Indian Treatise on Kamasutra*, Abhinav Publications, New Delhi, 2000.

Varadpande, M.L : *History of Indian Theatre*, Vols. I, II, III, Abhinav Publications, New Delhi, 2005.

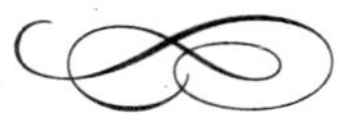

INDEX